Wise Words

FROM THE POWER PLANT KEEPER

Based on a True Story

Wise Words from the Power Plant Keeper

Copyright © 2016 Ginger K. Glomstead

Although *Wise Words from the Power Plant Keeper* is based on a true story, names, characters, places, and incidents have been changed and are either the product of the author's imagination, or are used fictitiously. Any resemblance to actual events, locales, or persons, living or dead, is entirely coincidental. Also it is pantheistic; no specific religion is supported by this fictional work.

Library of Congress Cataloging – in Publication Data
Library of Congress Control Number: 2014920416
ISBN: 0996094504
ISBN-13: 978-0-9960945-0-4
First eBook and Paperback published 2016

CBHE Publishing, a division of Center for Beauty and Health Excellence, www.CBHEpublishing.com

Wise Words

FROM THE POWER PLANT KEEPER

GINGER K. GLOMSTEAD

DEDICATION

This book is dedicated to all World War II vets, survivors and those civilians who gave their lives or were victims of that mass atrocity. The world is deeply indebted for your sacrifice. To honor all of you, this book is written so that we all may continue to thrive during our lifetime. Our current life issues are trivial compared to what all of you endured.

CONTENTS

ACKNOWLEDGEMENTS

Thank you to my mother, who inspired me to write
this book.

To all my reviewers, thank you for helping me in
getting this work completed.

Thank you to Kelsey Nornberg, for the beautiful
cover illustrations.

Totsy (Elizabeth Rose)

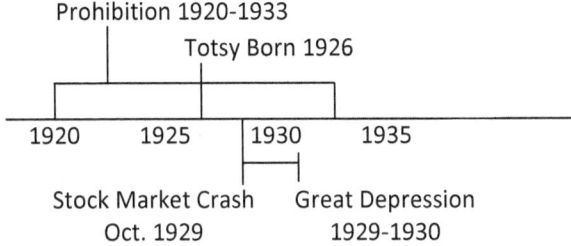

Prohibition 1920-1933
Totsy Born 1926
1920 1925 1930 1935
Stock Market Crash Great Depression
Oct. 1929 1929-1930

1 PASS THE TOTSY

She was born on the same day as Queen Elizabeth II, but their two lives could not have been more different. In fact, the only thing they had in common was their first names. At a young age, Elizabeth Rose was given the nickname of Totsy by her step-grandpa who loved her dearly. Totsy was born in a one-room cabin in northern Wisconsin that had a dirt floor and a wood burning potbelly stove. It wasn't much different from President Abraham Lincoln's boyhood home in Indiana.

Totsy was born in the U.S. into the poor immigrant farming way of life. She was raised during the times of the Roaring Twenties, when the world's economy was strong after World War I, manufacturing was flourishing and throngs of people were moving to the cities. Prohibition was in full swing, pushing alcohol production underground and spurring on gang activities such as the likes of Al Capone's. Totsy's extended family was one of the many farming families helping to feed and fuel the transition of an agrarian nation to one of manufacturing diversification. It was a tough life living in Merylville and to add to Totsy's plight, she was born out of wedlock.

Her mother was a caring, perfectionist, people-pleaser who chose to see the best in all people. She didn't have a bad bone in her body and her only downfall was thinking she could make Totsy's dad a better man. He abandoned them before Totsy was two years old.

Even so, Totsy's young life was filled with joy and love. She looked just like her mother, having dark, thick, wavy hair with cool, ice-blue eyes and milky white fair skin. Being the first born, just like her mother, she was doted upon by the women of her mother's family, showered with love and affection from all her aunts who dreamed of one day having a baby of their own.

Totsy was the oldest of three siblings born to first generation immigrants from Europe. Her maternal grandparents came over on a ship from Europe and were processed with the millions of other immigrants through Ellis Island. Her grandpa was a solider in the Hungarian Army and a tailor who migrated first to New York City then to the Midwest to take up farming. He died soon after from pneumonia and later grandma remarried step-Grandpa Friedrich.

Both Grandma and step-Grandpa Friedrich were kind, loving souls and hard workers. They both took a chance on moving to a new land that held promises of new opportunities. Grandpa Friedrich had a gentle gaze of unconditional love while grandma's was one of stern, no nonsense affection. She always had on a necklace of some sort whether beads or a gold cross to accent her floral long skirt dresses. Sometimes, she put sewing thread through her pierced ears so the holes wouldn't close up. Grandpa Friedrich usually wore a white button shirt with trousers and suspenders to work the fields. It was something he could easily put a blazer over to dress up if he went into town. They would often put others first before taking care of themselves.

One of the happiest days Totsy remembered was when Aunt Emmy got married to Grandpa Friedrich's cousin. Prohibition was still in effect but being of German and Hungarian ethnicity, they had family wine and beer recipes that they secretly made and so had ample alcohol to drink at the reception. These were the days of the women dressing as flappers with fringed dresses and headbands they wore over bob haircuts. The Charleston dance was all the rage. All in attendance would participate by singing, clapping or dancing. Totsy loved to hold hands with her two younger step-sisters or children of similar age, swirling in unison from left-to-right. The exhilaration of it all caused her to giggle a lot and put a big smile on her face for most of the day.

At this point Totsy had no idea of the riches that were possible in a person's life such as the queen inherited. Although Queen Elizabeth II was originally born into a family of affluence, her life changed when her uncle abdicated and her father became king, making her a princess. In the kingdom of royals lived farmers such as the family of Totsy's. The farmers worked hard to grow the foodstuffs needed to run a healthy, vibrant and strong kingdom where citizens were protected and allowed to flourish. But in contrast to Totsy's humble small town and farming family roots, the royals had power; power to rule, power over people, power to govern their sovereignty, power over their dominion.

Queen Elizabeth II was first a Lady born to the Duke and Duchess of York, part of the current dynastic ruling family of England and the British Monarch. She later became a princess when her father took over the British throne. Castles, estate homes, ornate horse drawn carriages, automobiles, and the finest of linens, foods and drink from around the world were the standard of living for royalty. They were high society and their daily work dealt with ceremonial and governmental duties for the people.

As a Lady and Princess, Queen Elizabeth II had parents just like Totsy, but she also had caregivers and servants who helped along the way in her upbringing. These individuals were not only responsible for ensuring the future queen stayed happy and healthy but also that she was protected and eventually schooled in all areas relevant to being a leader and ruler if she ever rose to that position; areas, such as, her realm of powers to rule and protect the kingdom in order to keep it abundantly flourishing.

Life as a royal was much different from a farmer although Totsy would also experience life-changing events at a young age. Her first life-changing event happened when her biological father, a third-generation saloon keeper, walked out on her and her mother.

Her mother remarried a very nice man and the whole family moved to town. August Roth Junior who was a carpenter by trade, also ran the local garage that sold new and used cars. The garage was in the town of Merylville and featured new Essex autos along with used cars and trucks such as Desoto's and Model-T Fords.

Merylville was the county seat and as such, the biggest town in the county with a main street which had the typical granary, cannery, hospital, butcher shop, clothing shops and a hotel near the train station. Totsy loved living there because of all the other kids that lived close by to play with her and Tulla. Her step-dad's service station was on the far end of Main Street on the outskirts of town.

August Jr. accepted Totsy whole heartedly although August's father, August Sr., did not. Tulla and Tetty were August Jr.'s daughters; Totsy was his step-daughter.

August Sr.'s ill-sentiment about Totsy and her mother was indiscreetly inferred by women in town too, who would point and whisper about Totsy, her mother, and her two step-sisters. They viewed her mother as a social climber and someone to be shunned for not meeting their societal standards. These jeers had a tinge of disrespect and were etched in Totsy's memory at a young age. She couldn't figure out why these women didn't like her and her mother but then when her step-father August was there, they were all nice like nothing was the matter. She just couldn't understand why she was felt to feel ashamed for being herself when just with her mother.

Everyday life was hard but even harder once the Great Depression hit. That October day in 1929 when the stock market crashed, it sent a ripple through the U.S. economy and dampened the emotional well-being of both the rich and poor. Everyone struggled to take it all in stride, continuing to contribute to the family, home, and community.

They took pride in all that they did and, on the rare occasion when they had a little extra money, tried to have some fun to relax and unwind by maybe scraping together a few cents to celebrate something.

It was during the hot, lazy days of summer, nearing dinner time when Totsy's life changed again forever. Her step-father had just gotten home from the garage and her mother was rushing around, trying to get dinner started. She hastily threw kerosene in the potbelly stove to light it when the stove combustion burst back at her, sending flames about the kitchen. Soon the wood framed house was engulfed in fire.

Her step-father and mother took the brunt of the explosion. August Jr., had been sitting closest to the stove. His face took the impact of the explosion, blinding him instantly and burning his skin on his face and arms. Her mother ran out of the house ablaze where she finally fell on the road, rolling to put the flames out.

The explosion and screams were heard by neighbors who came out of their homes to see what the commotion was about. The grown-ups believed that Totsy was the one who got her younger step-sisters out. They found them all outside, crying and watching the house burn, as they stood near their injured mother. Totsy was clutching her pillow, the angst on her face clearly visible with tears streaming down from her ice-blue eyes. The tears washed away a thin layer of the soot that had accumulated on her face which contrasted with her fair skin and thick, black hair.

The town's volunteer firemen came to fight the fire, but it was too late. As the flames of the fire were fueled by the wooden structure, the crackling of the blaze became deafening. Some of the firefighters and neighbors theorized there was maybe some gasoline mixed in with the kerosene to cause such an explosion. The horrifying site would remain etched in young Totsy's mind forever as she and her two younger step-sisters stood tearfully staring in disbelief.

Unfortunately, Totsy's bravery and valor left her parentless. With her step-father blinded and severely burned from the explosion and fire, he was unable to care for the young children. Her mother died at the Merylville hospital a few days later. Being a hero and parentless was very hard to comprehend at such a young age.

Totsy and her two younger step-sisters were immediately taken in to live by their maternal Friedrich grandparents. Grandma Friedrich quickly made three new outfits for the girls; their new Sunday best that they wore to their mother's funeral. At the funeral, Totsy saw flowers dancing about her mother's casket being carried by a misty figure. She thought it was her dead mother rearranging the flowers and she tried to tell the adults. Some believed her while others attribute it to an overactive imagination. August Jr.'s funeral was a few days later.

Being so young, it was difficult for her and her siblings to fully understand what had happened. They were parentless now. They didn't know the potential burden they would cause for others to take care of them. Her two younger step-sisters were adopted by Grandpa and Grandma Roth, the parents of their father whom Totsy's mother was married to at the time of the fire. Totsy was left in the care of her Friedrich grandparents, for she was the illegitimate daughter of a third-generation saloon owner. Children born out of wedlock were frowned upon in those days, as was the mother. And it was Grandpa Roth that had the problem with Totsy not being blood related. Totsy was still able to occasionally see her step-sisters for they all lived in the same farming community, although those visits were few and far between.

Totsy's mother was the eldest child in the family and so was already out of grandma and grandpa's house, making a family life for her own. With her mother's passing the responsibility fell upon Totsy's maternal grandparents and the extended family to take over responsibility for her care. But for Grandma and Grandpa Friedrich, Totsy was no burden. They showered her with love and affection just as she was one of their own. She put a twinkle in grandpa's eye and a smile on his face, even with her not being blood related to him. He loved his "little Totsy".

Living with Grandma and Grandpa Friedrich put instant stability and routine in young Totsy's life, helping her to heal her grieving heart. Grandma and grandpa had their own family, mostly boys, still living on the farm and in fact, Totsy had an Aunt Annabel who was four years older than her. They shared a bedroom and formed an instant, inseparable bond becoming more like sisters than aunt and niece.

Totsy was lucky enough to get some of her aunt's hand-me-down clothes for all of hers had been lost in the fire. She had a couple outfits to wear during the week and then the one grandma made for her, for her mother's funeral. It was only to be worn for Sunday church and special occasions. She also got dresses and long thick stockings that were donated to the local church. It wasn't until she was older that she started to wear pants on the farm. Most of the donated clothing was often stained and patched up or there would be missing or mismatched buttons.

Most days, grandma was up at sunrise to prepare breakfast for everyone. Helping grandma in the kitchen reminded her of being around her mother. She loved this quiet time of the morning and also helping Annabel, as she called her, gather the breakfast eggs. They had to make sure they closed up the chicken coops securely because the chickens and the eggs were favorite meals of the coyotes, wolves, and raccoons that roamed the countryside.

Usually by the time the young girls headed back to the house, they could smell the bread baking outside and when they went back inside it had enveloped the whole kitchen and crept into all corners of the house. Soon the smell of ham or bacon permeated the air and it was about that time her grandpa and uncles came in from milking the cows in the barn. Totsy's job was to fill the grape juice glasses. Being Hungarian immigrants, grandma always served everyone grape wine with the breakfast meal.

Totsy had other chores on her grandparents' farm which she happily completed. While her uncles and grandpa were out in the fields, she and Aunt Annabel fed some of the barn animals and cleaned their pens. Totsy loved the animals and the routine of caring for them gave her satisfaction and put structure in her life.

She was surprised by the personalities of the animals like when Pete the old plow-horse would bite her if she didn't give him a fresh cracked egg with his morning oats. And by how defensive the geese were whenever she entered their pen. They became mean and always tried to bite her. Her thick socks protected her legs but her sleeveless summer dresses left her arms exposed.

One day, a mean old goose was after her. Anger filled Totsy as she felt the repeated pinching of the beak bites on the back of her arms and legs. Totsy turned around in anger and swung the wooden rake handle at the gander. It hit him square on the side of his head and down he went. He lay motionless in the dirt. Totsy gasped in fright. Fearful tears filled her eyes as she dropped the rake and made a beeline out of the pen. She ran for help and found her Uncle Jake in the barn. He immediately stopped what he was doing when he heard her cries, "Uncle Jake! Uncle Jake!" He saw the distress on her face as she ran up to him, throwing her arms around his waist and burying her crying face into his torso.

"Uncle Jake" she cried, "I killed the goose."

He pulled her back and grabbed her by her shoulders and squarely looked into her eyes, "There, there Totsy. What's the matter?" He stroked the top of her head to try and get her to calm down.

"The geese were biting me." He could see the pink pinch marks up and down her arms. He stroked them gently as if to try to ease the pain. "And I took the rake handle and swung it at one. I killed him." Totsy burst into tears again, grabbing at his waist for comfort, "I killed him."

"There, there, let's go see what's going on with the geese." He took her by the hand and they walked over to the pen. Totsy was rubbing the residual tears away from her eyes as they turned the corner of the barn. Her stomach was tight and her breathing was shallow. Then to Totsy's surprise, all the geese were standing up. The one she had clobbered was all right.

Uncle Jake immediately teased her, "Well Totsy, the gander got your dander, but you didn't kill it."

Totsy was relieved but still felt horrible inside, thinking that she could have killed the animal. Fortunately for her, the goose revived and it was a scary, hard lesson that she learned not to be so quick to anger.

While Aunt Annabel was at school, Totsy helped grandma with the cooking and washing clothes. Grandma had to push her long sleeves up while washing the clothes in a wash tub. Suds and water would splash all over her embroidered white apron she wore over her long, full skirt. Her gold cross necklace would swing back and forth as she scrubbed them with lye soap and then rubbed the clothes up and down over a wash board. Totsy's job was to make sure the men's pants or the long skirts didn't hit the ground when grandma ran them through the rinse tub with the manual ringer.

Grandma Friedrich was a strong and very brave woman. One afternoon a black bear found its way up on the house porch and was trying to get in the kitchen screen door. After instructing Totsy and Annabel to go upstairs, she got the gun from above the living room mantel. It was already loaded. She quietly went out the front door and softly walked around the wrap-around porch. With the bear making all sorts of noise and scratching at the wood door, he didn't hear her come around the corner. With a quick click, a KABOOM was heard as the shotgun fired. She shot him dead with one bullet.

Totsy and Aunt Annabel also had secret responsibilities too. They were tasked with watching the moonshine stills and also keeping a look out for the sheriff. Doing whatever it took to keep the farm, Totsy's grandparents reverted to distilling spirits and fermenting wine and beer which they had learned how to do back in their old country. They then secretly sold these libations to the affluent in the area. These were tough economic times and they took advantage of the underground alcohol demands spurred on by prohibition. It was hushed that they helped supply the elite with homemade rhubarb, blackberry or grape wine along with beer, vodka and whiskey.

Totsy loved the family gatherings such as during corn husking time, weddings or barn raisings when grandpa, as she called him, would play his violin, grandma would play her singing saw or spoons and her uncles would play bass, banjos or jugs. A little bit of the homemade wine and beer would be sampled by the men. Grandpa would tap his foot and sing German and English songs. He would occasionally call out, "Come on Totsy! Give me a twirl!" She loved to twirl. Sometimes with Annabel, they would hold hands and circle left then right to the music. All the giggling and laughing as they played and danced filled Totsy with joy as was evident by the big smile on her face. These were happy, fun filled times for Totsy.

When Totsy was six, she joined her aunt in attending school. If they were lucky, a farmer in his wagon picked them up for a ride during their four mile walk to the one-room school house. The students ranged in age from 6-13 and the school served the local farming community for children up through the seventh grade. One boy, Bobby Schmidt, took a particular interest in Totsy. He sat behind her and to get her attention he often pulled her hair or socked her in the arm when they stood in line for their iodine pills. Even some of the local Native American children attended. One little Indian girl was blamed for bringing head lice to school that quickly spread to the other students. In those day's it was hard to get rid of lice, with the most popular treatment being to put kerosene on the infected scalp and hair to sleep in overnight followed by a head washing with lye soap in the morning.

Totsy's and her aunt's lunch boxes were often packed with lard sandwiches along with wormy apples which was the typical meal for all her fellow students. Even though the Great Depression had supposedly passed, it was still tough economic times in the U.S. The dust bowls of Oklahoma were raging and destroying crops across the farm belt region. Parents scrounged to feed their children what they could. Some children in the area did not even attend school for their parents needed them to work the fields and the farm.

Occasionally, Totsy and her aunt were so desperate for food that they ate raw potatoes dug up by hand from neighboring farmer's fields they passed going to and from school. If caught, they were scolded and sometimes ratted out by the farmer who complained to her Grandma and Grandpa Friedrich.

These were hard times, but happy, stable times for Totsy who was able to heal her heart and soul over the sadness she felt from the loss of her parents. Grandma told her to find something to be appreciative for each and every day. Some days, being thankful was a hard thing to do, but yet the only thing they had to keep going. Those were the days when they were so grateful for the dirt on their shoes that came from the fields that would sprout the seeds of optimism for a bountiful crop in the fall. Acknowledging their appreciation was about the only thing they had to hang on to that helped to keep them moving forward with their lives.

During these stressful times, Totsy and Aunt Annabel would catch grandma talking to God and deceased relatives. In her thick Hungarian accent, she would often be asking for help to get food on the table. Money was tight and it was all she could do to pull together enough to buy a sack of flour. Making distilled spirits on the side wasn't bringing in enough money to cover the farm mortgage and feed the family.

Eventually, Grandpa Friedrich was lucky enough to secure work as a scaler for an area logging company. His job was to determine how many planks could be made out of a tree. Grandma joined him as the cook for the logging camp. Totsy's uncles stayed to work the family farm while Totsy and Aunt Annabel went to live with grandma and grandpa at the logging camp. The four of them were bunked up in a one room house.

The winter was brutal at this logging camp. Not only was it below zero cold, but there was also a lot of snow that made the retrieval of the trees difficult. The horses were wading in snow up to their bellies and the production of planks was behind schedule. Then it was discovered by the logging camp boss that Totsy was not the biological daughter of Grandma and Grandpa Friedrich. He gave them an ultimatum; get rid of Totsy to keep their jobs or lose their jobs.

It broke grandma and grandpa's hearts that the camping boss would not consider the hard-economic times of the Great Depression and the difficult predicament the grandparents were in. They took on work at the logging camp to help cover the payments on the farm. Not only did grandma lose her eldest daughter, but now she had to give up her eldest granddaughter.

Her grandparents openly talked about Totsy and her fate. With her two younger step-sisters, Tulla and Tetty, already gone to live with the Roth family, it was decided she temporarily would go live with her older Aunt Emmy before being put into foster care. This was the start of the "Pass the Totsy."

The birds chirped around Totsy who stood motionless in the logging camp yard. Grandma Friedrich got down on one knee to say good-bye to her. A light spring breeze swept a few hairs about Totsy's face as she held back her tears. She was putting up a brave front, not wanting to cry in front of Aunt Annabel nor the men milling about the yard.

It was hard for Totsy to understand why once again she was being separated from her family. Her stoic front was covering up her fear as she submitted to the situation. She sat quietly in the front seat of the car. Being just tall enough to peer out the window she gave a last look at Grandma Friedrich and Aunt Annabel as Aunt Emmy drove away. At seven years old, Totsy was once again tossed to face a life of new challenges.

DEFINITIONS

Powerisms are concepts that are full of force or energy. They are active and potent and influence an individual on many levels such as physical, mental and emotional and often times have more than one aspect. **Power Tools** are actions that can be taken to positively propel or influence an individual to move forward in achieving their goals.

POWERISMS

* **Power of Love:**   Loving influences can shape your life. Through love you can positively influence another's life. You should always come from a place of love. Sometimes other forces are at work and love just isn't enough.

* **Power of Fear:**   Fear can hold you back or propel you forward in times of distress. It can also protect you.

* **Power of Survival:**   Any event you survive gives you more references to draw upon. Sometimes you repeat experiences until you learn. With each experience, you accumulate strength and stamina.

* **Power to Heal:**   Just being in the presence of someone who offers unconditional love can heal. People can heal themselves too through meditative prayers or in changing their health habits.

* **Power of the Heart:**   Your heart is most powerful at manifesting and is intricately connected to your mind and to a higher knowing.

When the decision is made to follow the heart, it is usually the correct decision.

* **Power of Anger:** Anger can change a person's life forever. An individual needs to control their response to mitigate the possible negative repercussions of the outcome. If the response is done hastily, as in a reaction without thought, it can cause regret.

POWER TOOLS

* **Appreciation:** Find something each day to be appreciative for in a way that easily incorporates into your daily routine. Each thing you are grateful for is a blessing. This simple practice gives your life a sense of fulfillment and signals the universe to send you more blessings.

* **Creative Expression:** Creative activities can include dancing, laughing, hanging out with friends, painting or anything creative that allows your mind to shift focus and the answers to come through. These activities instill a sense of joy while reducing stress and anxiety.

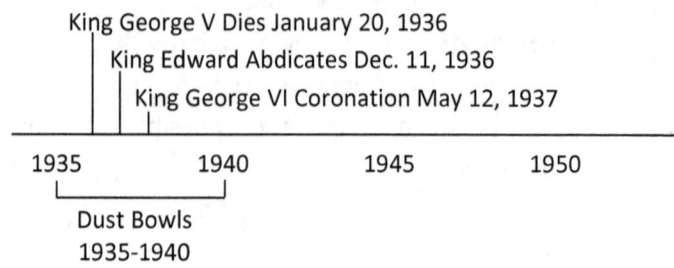

King George V Dies January 20, 1936
King Edward Abdicates Dec. 11, 1936
King George VI Coronation May 12, 1937

1935   1940   1945   1950

Dust Bowls
1935-1940

2 JADE

Totsy was moved around to eight different foster homes by the time she was 12 years old. Some she was at for only three months before being moved on to the next foster home. Although she was given food and shelter, she was worked hard for the simplest necessity of having a roof over her head. These homes lacked love and encouragement. The U.S. economy was still somewhat struggling after the Great Depression and the Dust Bowl was happening in the Great Plains region so there were many others who also lacked loving support.

With Totsy being in county foster care, it was as if the farmers were double dipping because they were not only reimbursed $3 a month for giving her food and shelter, but also used her to work in their fields. She felt like a slave. If she were still living with grandma and grandpa, she would have been doing the same but received love, encouragement and affection from them. During harvest season, she was passed around to whatever farmers needed her to help with babysitting or the crop harvesting. Once the cucumbers were all picked, it was off to the green bean farm to harvest the beans.

Foster family life was cruel and hard. Her daily communications consisted mostly of "Do this" or "Do that" or "Don't do this or that" by the foster elders. She remembered that at one of the first foster homes she was crying for her mom. The foster mother in frustration slapped her hard and loudly scolded her, "Your mother is dead!"

From the impact of the blow, her vision went white and it stunned her. She immediately stopped crying and never cried for her mother again.

Another year, the family she stayed with was so poor she actually had to wear two right foot shoes. After wearing the shoes for a few days and getting the leather wet a few times, the leather stretched to accommodate her left foot. The mother of that particular household did all she could to scrape up a few cents to buy some flour to cook with for the week. Loving affection wasn't a priority when there were hungry mouths to feed. They made do with what they had.

But Totsy never complained. It never did her any good to complain. If she did, she was accused of being ungrateful on top of being unloved by the foster parents she stayed with. That was how life was during the Great Depression. She was ever so grateful to have clothes to help keep her warm and a roof over her head to protect her.

When the field work or the daily chores were done, Totsy often made her way out to the solitude of the fields to privately sit in nature for a while. It was here that she pondered her fate, questioning why life had turned out to be so cruel to her.

At one foster farm, she had a favorite boulder she liked to sit upon. It was too large for the farmer's horses to move and they just worked the field around it. She always carried a big broken tree branch with her that she clicked on the ground as she wandered her way out to her favorite spot. The country breezes would stir her fly-away hair about her face and the warmth of the sunshine penetrated her skin, gently embracing her during her reprieve from her unhappy circumstances. During her time of solitude, birds such as juncos, sparrows, and red-wing black birds or butterflies such as monarch or cabbage would often gather around her. They were her friends and she welcomed their company. She was comforted in the joy of the melodic, chirping bird songs and her favorite was the song of the chickadees. She felt gentle, protective, kindness from the whimsical fluttering of the butterflies that seemed to effortlessly hover by her as if a loved one was keeping a watchful eye over her.

One day the birds were all upset, chirping away in a cautious taunt. A bobcat came out of the thicket. Fright overtook Totsy at the site of him. The cat stopped in his tracks and they made eye contact. Her breathing became shallow, her heartbeat was beating rapidly and the birds were chirping wildly around them. Anxious fear overtook her as she reacted instinctively and took her big stick and hit it against the big boulder several times, screaming out loud "Get out of here! Shoo! Go AWAY!" The noise and the motion of her swings combined with the birds excitability caused the bobcat to turn and continue on the other way.

Being in foster care, Totsy felt she was treated as a hired slave, a second rate person. She never received any love or affection from these families. She was worked hard and tolerated for existing. It was a hard, lonely existence for a young child. And being poor wasn't just her plight, but the plight of all who were living through the Great Depression.

At the seventh foster home, Totsy was blessed with living in town. Harvest time was over and the farmers didn't need her. Totsy loved living in town. It reminded her of when she lived there when her mother was alive, before the house fire. Life was much easier there. Most homes had electricity and phones.

Merylville even had a movie theater where, on rare occasions, Totsy was able to go. Movies helped take away the worries of the day of the theater-goers who also identified with the plight of the hero or heroine, and showed that the characters had villains too. The movies allowed a safe and relaxing escape from the hardships and the woe of the economy and the war that was looming. Hollywood seemed like a land of magic to Totsy.

She started to attend Merylville High School and was lucky enough that some of the farm kids from the one-room school house were going there too, like her Aunt Annabel and Bobby Schmidt. She did however form some strong bonds with new friends at school who empathized with her plight. One was a sweet girl named Rachel that Totsy referred to as "Rae". Rae and Totsy could always be seen eating lunch together. Her family was doing a little better than most and so her mother sometimes packed cookies which Rae gladly shared with Totsy. From their conversations, Totsy gleamed that Rae's family was much more loving and stable than the foster family homes she was thrown into.

The Dee foster family she lived with was nothing special. The husband worked at the area egg plant as a supervisor. Mr. Dee had a slight limp that was the result of a farm accident when he was a young boy. The farm tractor got stuck in some mud and as they tried to rock it out, it fell over and one of the wheels pinned his leg, breaking it in two places. It didn't heal straight and as a result he had a bit of a limp when he walked.

Mr. Dee did marry though, his school sweetheart. He and his wife had an amicable, mundane sort of existence. They had two younger boys that occasionally Totsy watched for them. But for the most part Mrs. Dee was usually around, handling most of the caregiving and cooking for the family. Totsy of course helped with cleaning up the dishes and with laundry as well. It was a stable, quiet environment that Totsy felt safe in but, as was the norm, it lacked the closeness and joy of a tight-knit loving family. It was understood, she wouldn't be staying with them very long.

Next door to this family though, lived an old eccentric neighbor lady. Through her thick British accent, she introduced herself to Totsy, "My name is Mrs. Jane Elliott but you can call me Jade. That's what my deceased husband used to call me." This woman turned out to be a blessing for Totsy, a loving grounding influence to her. Jade had beautiful deep green eyes and wore a gold chain necklace with a carved jade pendant that was as big as Totsy's tiny fist. She still wore full layered skirts with long-sleeved shirts, just like Totsy's Grandma Friedrich wore.

Totsy was instantly drawn to her. There was a sense of loving serenity she felt in her presence. There was calmness and caring she hadn't quite felt before.

The kids in town mocked and ridiculed Jade because she was different. One day Totsy was approaching the Dee home, when two boys rode by on bicycles. They were chasing the train heading into the city center station. They taunted out, "Hi crazy lady" to Jade who was raking the autumn leaves out of her flower beds. They called her crazy because she had a funny accent and dressed old fashioned. Jade just waved at them and responded, "Be careful boys." They didn't understand her at all and didn't take the time to get to know her like Totsy knew her.

Jade immigrated with her husband and two sons to the U.S. after the First World War. Her husband was a successful merchant who took long trips over the vast oceans to distant countries such as India, China and Japan. And from those trips, he shared with Jade the beauty he found in the different cultures. In fact, the jade necklace she wore daily was a gift from him on one of his trips abroad.

With her two sons out on their own and now a widow, Jade filled her days by helping out at church, working in her yard and gardens and re-reading the many books in her library. Totsy was a welcomed diversion to her day. One she looked forward to by baking boat sail biscuits, which were sugar cookies cut in triangles in honor of her husband's seafaring days. It was during these visits that Totsy felt loved and welcomed. Jade expanded Totsy's education to cover topics not covered in school which Jade had knowledge of through her extensive book collection and her husband's travels. And every day, Jade always had something special to share, just with Totsy.

Totsy loved being around Jade. Jade always greeted her with a warm smile that emanated free flowing, loving, kindness and often with open arms to wrap Totsy in a big hug. Totsy couldn't wait to get home from school to spend time with Jade. She loved every minute they spent together and the stories she shared with her that expanded her awareness of the world. The attention Jade gave her was focused, engaging, and caring. But to those on the outside like the Dee's and other neighbors, they thought Jade to be an old, lonely woman that was over-indulging Totsy to fill her loneliness.

During their afterschool tea time visits, they typically sat at Jade's kitchen table that was pushed against the wall under two double hung windows. Jade usually had thrown something out for the birds to eat such as old bread and it gave them something to look at while they conversed.

"So how was your day dear?" Jade would inquire of Totsy who would share with her different things that happened to her.

"Bobby was pulling my hair again at school today. He even pushed me and pulled at my coat causing me to fall in the snow."

Jade just chuckled, "Did you ever think that maybe he likes you Totsy? Boys sometimes have a hard time letting a girl know they like them."

Totsy pondered Jade's suggestion for a moment then Jade asked, "What did his eye's look like? Were they playful or angry?"

"He was smiling at me."

"The eyes are the window to the soul. He likes you

and is just trying to get your attention. You're just having a hard time expressing yourself to him. Next time he pulls your hair, instead of getting mad, state your feelings about what he does and why you feel that way. Then add what you want him to do in the future or else there will be a consequence."

"A consequence?" Totsy questioned.

"Yes, say that you know he is doing it because he likes you and if he doesn't stop, you will say it out loud for others to hear. Then he will most likely stop."

Totsy was intrigued with Jade's suggested approach on how to handle Bobby's hair-pulling.

Jade continued, "Write out what you plan to say and practice it a few times. After repeating it 3-5 times it should be an automatic response so you can deliver your message succinctly."

"Can I have pencil and paper to write it out right now?" Totsy felt a sense of empowerment from Jade's insightful suggestion and wanted to get it right.

"Why sure, dear child."

Jade helped her write out her response. Totsy went back to the Dee household eager to review her response and commit it to memory. She was feeling invigorated and uplifted, that with any situation she was unhappy with, she had an option to change it.

Jade often told Totsy wonderful stories of faraway lands along with firsthand accounts of her life in the United Kingdom and of her husband's service in the Royal Navy. She shared with Totsy tales of the life of royalty and the dynastic ruling families of the world that went way back in history. How there were kings and queens, princes and princesses in Europe and how they lived. How their lives were ones of opulence and riches gained by several centuries of warfare and dynasties. She shared how for centuries, ruling families married other ruling families to gain advantages and protection.

Totsy particularly loved Jades stories on Queen Elizabeth I. Not only did they share the same first name, but also Queen Elizabeth I took over ruling from her step-sister Mary who wasn't so kind to her. Totsy could relate to not being accepted by the way her step-grandfather August Roth Sr. had treated her. She also loved how strong Queen Elizabeth I was, taking over where her father left off with expanding the British Empire and commanding a fleet of ships that sailed the oceans.

All these stories that Jade shared took Totsy away to lands she never dreamt of before. She had studied U.S. history in school which included how the U.S. split from England during the revolutionary war, but Jade's stories brought a depth and awareness that Totsy hadn't perceived previously. These were fascinating stories that filled Totsy with hope and carried her far away from her hard life as an orphan and a foster child.

One December day when Totsy was at her house for her usual biscuits cut into boat sails, Jade showed her a newspaper article about the King of England, Edward VIII, who was abdicating his throne for an American divorcee that he had proposed to, Wallace Simpson. The article had a black and white picture of him giving his speech that was broadcast by radio stations around the world, stating that his brother the Duke of York would take over the throne. Totsy had no idea who these people were but could tell they were not from her part of the world. Jade was sure to point out to Totsy that Edward must truly love Wallace to give up his throne. "You too, can have true love one day Totsy, and a loving family of your own, just like I had with my husband."

"Speaking of family," Jade paused as she looked out the kitchen windows at the birds scampering about looking for some bread crumbs to eat. "All day I've had this feeling that something is wrong with one of the grandchildren. I don't know what it is, but something just isn't right."

BRINGG, BRINGG, went the phone on Jade's kitchen wall. It was usually one of Jade's sons calling to check-in on her. It was nearing dinner time and it was Totsy's cue that it was time to go to the Dee household for the night.

Jade answered, "Hi dear" then briefly listened. "What happened?"

Totsy gave a look of concern toward Jade as she gathered up her school books and slid on her winter coat.

"Joseph has polio?" Jade questioned. Her intuitive inkling was correct.

Totsy gave a comforting touch on Jade's arm as she exited. It was a sad end to her visit and Totsy thought that she would maybe check back in on Jade after dinner.

That night in bed after giving thanks for the things she was grateful for, Totsy made a special mention for a speedy recovery for Jade's grandson. Then she shifted her thoughts to the article Jade showed her on King Edward VIII. She let her mind wander as she imagined living in a castle and what it would be like being the ruler of her own kingdom. She imagined how she would look wearing the royal regalia, how she would hold court, and how she would command her audiences and her kingdom. Often times these thoughts would carry over into her dreams.

As their visits continued, Jade took in all of Totsy's worries and concerns, counseling her a little bit regarding matters she was encountering as part of her journey in life. She was very encouraging to Totsy as well. Always telling her she could do anything she set her mind to. It was as if Totsy's visits to Jade were a continuation of her personal schooling.

When she could, Jade tied in spiritual truths that applied to whatever situation Totsy found herself in. Wisdoms, from various world religions, were found in the many books that Jade kept in her library. She accumulated the books over the years when her husband traveled. They gave her an understanding of the countries her husband was traveling to and made their conversations on his travels much more engaging. Jade found comfort in re-reading the books over the years since her husband passed.

Several of the books were on long-ago leaders that formed the religions of Buddhism, Hinduism and Taoism as well as Judaism, Islam and Christianity. These leaders spoke of spiritual truths such as what you think you become and that one should watch their thoughts and actions. Totsy was surprised by so many similar tenets in the various religions but also to learn that Moses was not only a key figure in Christianity but also in Islam and Judaism.

Jade shared with Totsy that thoughts and words have the power to create and that they can set the direction of her life.

"You have to choose your words wisely, child" she

schooled Totsy. "The words you use can positively or negatively impact your life. The emotion you feel when you express words is all powerful as well. Always try to focus on things that bring you joy or happiness."

Tapping on Totsy's temple area, she continued, "Your imagination and thoughts have the power to attract all you desire, especially if you pull those desires down here," Jade pointed to the center of her chest near her heart. "Be careful what you think and say, and how you say it, dear."

Totsy didn't quite understand that ultimately she would create her own life and that one day she could have everything that she desired, but she did know how to dream. Lying in bed, she often fantasized of becoming a princess herself, of living in a castle, and wearing beautiful clothes along with tiaras and jewels. She pictured herself riding in fancy horse drawn carriages or big cars, and of her prince in royal regalia accompanying her on their ceremonial duties.

The frigid January air kept Jade inside all day. Totsy let herself in the back door when she saw no sign of Jade at her kitchen table. Eerie silence filled the house except for the ticking sounds from the various clocks echoing about the house.

"Jade?" She called out as she pulled her wool mittens off and began to search for her.

"I'm in here dear" Jade called back. She was in her library by the fireplace. She had started to push off her thick quilt that was draped over her lap when Totsy found her. The loud tick of the mantle clock could be heard resounding throughout the room.

"No, no. Just sit Jade," Totsy ordered her. "I will

get the tea."

Jade sat back down and Totsy helped her put the quilt back over her lap.

"How was your day, dear?"

Totsy was already out of the room but called back, "I'll be right back. I'll get the tea first."

"Ok, dear."

Several minutes later, Totsy returned with the tea service tray.

"So how was your day, dear?"

In a matter-of-fact manner, while pouring the tea, Totsy shared, "The weather is cold, school was boring and Bobby Schmidt is irritating. How about yours?"

Jade chuckled, "I still think he likes you. What did he do today?"

"He was doing the fake shoulder tap."

"Did you ever get to express your feelings to him?"

"No, there are always too many people around and I don't want to make an embarrassing scene."

"Well, try to talk to him. Do you ever see him outside of school?"

"I usually see him hanging out at the train station after school."

"Well stop by and say 'hi'. Ask him what he is doing."

Totsy shrugged her shoulders, "I'll try, but I don't know what good it will do."

"Oh dear," Jade smiled at Totsy then took a sip of tea. "I took advantage of the cold day by staying warm inside and reading some of the books my husband bought me."

"Like what?" Totsy asked as she got comfy in one of the library chairs near Jade.

Jade was studying the necklace her husband had given her. "Did I ever tell you that the carving in this pendant is the Chinese symbol for love?"

Totsy shook her head side-to-side, "No" and then took a sip of her tea.

"That's why my husband gave me the nickname Jade. It was his play on words on my first name of Jane and his love for me. After he gave me the necklace, he started to affectionately call me Jade, his jade, his love."

Totsy could tell Jade was having one of those reminiscent kind of days. She picked up a book that was on the table, "So, is that what you were reading today?"

"I was re-reading this book on Taoism which I got when my husband went to China. It was on this trip that he purchased this necklace for me. It's a Chinese belief system built around the premise that Tao is the driving force and the source of everything that exists."

Jade took a sip of her tea. "You know they built the Great Wall of China over several centuries. At first it was made up of earth rammed between wooden structures during the early time of the warring fractioned states that made up China. Then later, during the Ming Dynasty, they used carved stone and brick to connect the walls. They built it to serve as protection against the Mongols and it took a lot of planning and workers to build it. What determination those emperors had in order to complete such a large scale endeavor."

Jade had Totsy grab a couple more books down from her bookshelf. Her discussion carried over into other religions of the world and their monarchies such as in Japan and India. She shared how these religions spoke of an unseen energy they referred to as chi, qi or prana and she opened the books to show Totsy illustrations depicting this as well as energy fields found in and around the body in areas called chakras. Jade explained that chakras had different emotions and colors associated with them and could be balanced or unbalanced, opened or closed. Also, that there were meridian lines that connected with these energy fields surrounding the body that were called auras.

She pointed out how these spiritual truths and energy systems were similar to things found in Christianity, as she pointed to a picture of Jesus hanging on her library wall with his halo vibrantly shining around his head. Then she pointed to her own chest and told Totsy, "You have the same spark inside you."

All of this was whimsical, out of this world information that Totsy found fascinating. She knew there were different types of churches all based on Christianity because, as a foster kid, she had been in Catholic, Lutheran, and Methodist churches for services so it was easy for her to believe Jade's stories of different religions with different but similar beliefs to be true. Plus, as Jade had already shared with her, Moses was mentioned in Islam, Judaism and Christianity.

Jade shared with her another book about a Japanese belief system called Buddhism. She shared with Totsy how a long time ago there lived a Japanese spiritual leader called Buddha that spoke of eight truths: Right Belief, Right Intentions, Right Speech, Right Actions, Right Livelihood, Right Endeavoring,

Right Mindfulness, and Right Concentration. Another key principle was living in the 'now'. These Buddhists practiced meditation and cultivating a higher wisdom and discernment. Some who practiced took on a monastic life similar to the nuns of the Catholic Church in which Totsy was raised. Totsy was starting to see how these beliefs and practices related to Christianity and what Jade had basically been sharing with her all along such as to watch what she says and thinks.

Jade was also very adamant about telling Totsy to not attend séances which were all the rage of the day. Some ladies in town organized one after the death of one lady's husband.

"They're opening themselves up to negativity" Jade said. "Don't ever be a part of that, Totsy. You only want to attract good spirits to you and sometimes they bring in bad spirits. You want to shield yourself and keep your energy as pure as possible."

The conversation with Jade caused the hairs on Totsy's arms to rise up and she quivered because she had a flashback to her mother's funeral when, as a young child, she saw the spirit of her mother rearranging the flowers.

"Watch it with the psychics too. They tap into your energy to retrieve information and you may not agree with their interpretation of things."

Jade closed the books she had in her lap and reclined back in her chair. Her mood changed to being very serious. She turned her head, while pointing at her chest and solemnly spoke, "Just remember Totsy, all the answers are inside. Be a seeker of truth, but always go within for the answers."

On a bright, blue-sky, spring day, Totsy took her time walking home from school. As she walked, she pondered some of the events of her day. Her thoughts shifted over to some of her conversations with Jade. She remembered how Jade suggested she try to run into Bobby Schmidt outside of school and she immediately changed her course to cut over to the train station.

The train station was a favorite hangout of the kids in town, for those who dreamed of the faraway places the trains went to like Milwaukee and Chicago. Bobby and some other boys were smoking cigarettes and hanging out at the end of the platform. The stationmaster and porter were busy loading the mail bags and some other goods on the train. Totsy bravely approached them as she recalled the statements to say to kindly confront him.

"Hi Bobby, what are you guys doing?"

"None of your business" he snapped back. He nervously took a big drag of his cigarette.

One of the boys ribbed him, which also made Totsy uneasy, "Ooo, she likes you."

Bobby's face started to get red. Totsy got angry with their teasing,

"Oh, shut up you guys. He likes me, because he's always pulling my hair and doing the fake shoulder tap which makes me mad," she boldly stated.

Just then the conductor made the 'All Aboard' call and the clang of the steam engine bell began to signal the train's departure.

Bobby's face turned a brighter shade of red and flushed down his neck. Totsy continued, "I don't like getting mad, so I'm just trying to be nice and maybe he will stop."

Chugga chugga chugga, chugga chugga chugga, the steam engine train was exiting the station as the other boys all threw down their cigarette butts to stomp them out.

One of the boys gave Bobby one last jab, "Way to go, lover boy."

Bobby gave him and Totsy a stern look as he took one last drag of his cigarette. It was like he was pondering what to say then he diverted his eyes to the train. Without saying a word he threw his cigarette on the ground and took off running.

The stationmaster called out after the boys to stop because he knew they were going to be illegally boarding the train to take a free ride.

The other boys were already inside the open train car, as Bobby ran alongside the train. It was picking up speed, CHUG A LUG, CHUG A LUG, CHUG A LUG, but Bobby managed to grab the hand rails. They helped him inside where he turned to look back at Totsy. He stood leaning on the side of the open door with his hands in his pants pockets. With the final whistle call of CHOO, CHOOOOO, Totsy gave a wave. Bobby actually pulled a hand out and gave her a reciprocal two finger wave.

Totsy hurried her way to Jade's house to tell her what happened. Jade greeted her with her customary upbeat, "Hello Totsy! Did you have a good day at school today?"

As Totsy entered Jade's house, she blurted out, "I did what you said today!"

"What's that?"

"I went to see if I could catch Bobby after school at the train station."

"And how did it go?"

"I asked what he was doing and the boys teased us. Then I said that I knew he liked me. He got all mad at me, but didn't say anything."

"What did his eyes tell you?" Jade asked.

"He's seemed kind of embarrassed, maybe taken off guard."

"See, the eyes don't lie, they are the window to his inner feelings. He likes you. You exposed him in front of his friends. The truth is out and maybe he will leave you alone or be nicer to you from now on."

"Yeah, I hope so. He did wave to me from the train afterwards."

"Well that's good news too." Jade patted the side of Totsy's face. "You did well in conveying your thoughts and feelings to him. Now the ball is in his court." With a wave of her hand, Jade started to exit the kitchen,

"Come, I have something for you in the living room."

Totsy followed her to the front of the house where she saw a big box of stuff Jade had gathered up and placed by the door.

Fearing that Jade was moving, Totsy cried out, "What is all this stuff?"

"Oh, dear child," Jade smiled as she stepped toward the box. "Today, I've been busy doing some spring cleaning. Its stuff I've been holding onto that I need to let go. They remind me of things that have happened in my life and I no longer want to be reminded of those feelings."

"Feelings, like what?" Totsy asked.

"Well," Jade began, "like this broken figurine." The figurine was of a ballerina twirling on one leg with her arms in the air. Except that one arm had broken off above the elbow.

"My sons were wrestling in the house one day which they weren't supposed to do. My one son hit his head on the edge of a table which knocked him out and caused a big cut in his forehead."

Totsy listened intently, seeing the strain on Jade's face as she recounted the event.

"This figurine hit the floor and I don't know why I hang on to it. Every time I look at it, it hurts me inside. My stomach gets tight and it reminds me of that terrible day. We had to take him to the doctor and he got stitches in his forehead."

Jade rustled some papers in the box. "These were the payments we made to the doctor. I've been hanging on to these for 20 years."

Jade brushed back the fly-away hairs from around her face. Recalling this event stressed her somewhat.

"And then this crocheted doily was given to me by someone I no longer associate with, Myrtle. Myrtle always had to have things her way and everything we did was what she wanted to do. The one time I needed her to help me get my husband's car to the service station, she was unavailable all day. I found out from Mrs. Jameson that Myrtle wasn't busy at all. She saw her downtown at one of the clothing shops and that Myrtle had been shopping all day."

Discussing Myrtle stirred up a little anger in Jade who felt unsupported by someone she thought was a friend.

"It's not very Christian to bear a grudge but I prefer to think our friendship had run its course. I don't need to be a rug and walked over repeatedly just because it is convenient for someone else. Friendship is a two-way street."

Dropping the doily at the side of the box, Jade moved on to the next item.

"I found this bundle of letters up in a chest in the attic too."

Her mood became more somber.

"I had completely forgotten I still had them in the bottom of a trunk we moved from England. The man that sent them to me died a tragic death at sea. I loved him in a romantic way. I met him before my husband but I just can't hang on to them anymore. When I look at them, I wonder what my life would have been like with him and it makes me sad. I feel it conflicts with the feelings of love and gratitude I have for having such a caring, loving, devoted husband for so many years. And I just have to let it go."

Jade began to place the items back in the box.

"You will see, Totsy, when you are older. You will need to purge your life of people and things that no longer serve you. Things that you have been hanging on to that sap and steal your power from you. You need to keep the inside of your house clean and clear just like you need to keep your inside thoughts clean and clear. Anything you dwell upon that holds negative feelings for you can block you and hold you back. You need to release these thoughts and feelings to be free to attract what you desire. Put your focus on what you want, not on what you don't want or things that have caused you pain. You need to put yourself in a place of joy. You have had a hard life my child, but you can change all that and make a better life for yourself."

Then Jade picked up a small embroidered table runner which had some things wrapped up in it.

"And this is what I have for you," she said as she

unwrapped the items. It was a beautiful silver plated vanity set of a hand-mirror, boar bristle brush and comb with inlaid pearl.

"Oh my gosh, Jade! These are so beautiful!" exclaimed Totsy. She picked up each piece to examine them more closely.

Jade smiled as she saw the joy on Totsy's face. "My husband brought these back from one of his trips. I never used them and, at my age, I don't think I ever will."

Totsy put the vanity pieces down and gave her a big hug,

"Thank you, thank you, thank you!" Totsy stood back looking at them on the bench, "I don't think I have ever been given such a nice gift."

"You deserve them dear and I know you will take good care of them. I hope they will always remind you of me."

"What are you going to do with all this stuff?"

"Get rid of it. Some things I will burn, like these papers. Other things, I am just going to throw in the trash. There's no sense in letting the negative energy spread to someone else," Jade chuckled.

A couple of evenings later, Mr. and Mrs. Dee broke the news that with the weather finally warming up, Totsy was to move to another farming foster family. This should have been good news that it was Aunt Evie's farm she was moving to, but Totsy was upset at being separated from Jade. She ran to Jade the moment she learned she was going to a different foster home, back out in the countryside. Tears were streaming down her face, and the angst was clearly visible. She threw her arms around Jade and hugged her as tight as she could. She didn't want to leave Jade nor the mutual love and affection between the two of them.

Jade calmed her down and reassured her everything would be alright. "Just remember Totsy, there are several steps we take along our path. Choose your path. Where do you want to end up? And plan how you will get there."

The day of Totsy's departure arrived. Totsy was in a solemn mood even though the birds were singing up a storm on such a beautiful, sunny day in May. As Totsy and Jade sat down at Jade's kitchen table she fixated on some sparrows that were hopping around the rose bushes by the driveway. Jade studied the sadness on Totsy's face as she grabbed the tea kettle off the cast iron stove. She already had the tea cups and biscuits on the table.

"Are you all packed and ready to go?"

Totsy's eyes welled up with tears, "Yeah, I did most of it last night."

Jade put her arm around young Totsy's shoulders. She felt the sadness in the child's body, as Totsy embraced her back with all her strength. A little part of Jade's heart broke too, as she was going to have to let Totsy go.

Jade pulled back from Totsy, "There, there young thing." She swept the streaming tears off Totsy's face. "Everything will be alright. As I told you last night, I'm not leaving you. You will still be able to come see me when you are in town."

Jade's words weren't very reassuring to Totsy. She was consumed with gloom at being separated from the one she wanted to be with the most and loved dearly. Jade was the loving, mother figure she desired so desperately to have in her life.

Totsy sat quietly at the table; her tears subsiding somewhat. She was so upset. She couldn't even eat the biscuits Jade had set out on the table for her. Jade noticed the newspaper on the counter that she had folded to an article she specifically wanted to show Totsy.

"Here, this article will make your day Totsy."

The article featured a black and white photograph of the newly coronated King of England, King George VI, his wife, Queen Elizabeth of England and their Princess daughters Elizabeth and Margaret.

Jade stood by Totsy's side as she glanced at the photo, "See, Totsy," Jade said as she pointed to the young Princess Elizabeth, "You were born on the same day as Princess Elizabeth, the same day as English Royalty."

Bearing a smile of surprise, Totsy snatched the paper from Jade's hand. She examined the picture up close and began to read the article out loud.

"Princess Elizabeth was born a Lady. Her grandfather was King George V. His eldest son Edward was King for only a short time before leaving to marry American divorcee Wallace Simpson."

Totsy's mood was improving. "I remember you showed me the other articles."

"Yes, just remember anything is possible, dear. I know you are upset about living with your aunt, but remember, it's just a stepping stone on the way. It is not your final destination. You just need to put yourself where you want to be in order to have the opportunity to achieve your dreams. You can achieve anything you desire. You really have a beautiful spark

41

within you, dear child."

Totsy understood Jade's last comment to mean that she had a shiny disposition. She didn't fully comprehend what Jade meant by her spark.

Still sitting at the kitchen table, Jade draped a towel around Totsy's shoulders then handed her a wooden spoon, "I crown you Queen Totsy of Merylville!"

Jade's deep green eyes laughed with glee at seeing the young Totsy who proudly struck a pose and relished the thought that she could one day, possibly, be a queen.

With Totsy's change in mood her appetite returned and she began to munch on the biscuits. Jade left the kitchen and soon returned with a necklace dangling in her hands. She held it in front of Totsy who beamed at the sight of it. It was a small jade pendant on a gold chain, similar to the one worn by Jade. But unlike Jade's, there was also three small tiger eye stones that accented the tear-shaped stone.

As Jade put the necklace on Totsy she said, "Know that deep inside you always have the power within you. The power to be strong and to create the life you desire. Your strength and determination will always carry you through." Totsy was fixated on Jade and her words.

Jade smiled as she positioned the pendant over Totsy's heart. Next, she placed both hands on Totsy's shoulders and looked her squarely in the eyes, "Remember the spark I told you about?"

Totsy nodded her head in acknowledgement. Jade pointed to her chest, "It is right inside your heart. Use your noggin and put it there." Jade tapped Totsy's temple area "First in mind," then tapped the center of her chest, "then in reality. Feel what you want in your heart."

Jade stood straight, still looking down at young Totsy. "You have such a beautiful light within you. Remember, dear Totsy, your thoughts and words can positively set the direction of your life forever."

POWERISMS

* **Power of Words:** Written and spoken words can set the direction of one's life, either positively or negatively and most definitely affects others on a daily basis.

* **Power of Thoughts:** Thoughts can be the catalyst to change. Some repetitive thoughts are a lesson to be learned. Once the lesson is learned the thoughts cease. Repetitive thoughts, if not controlled can causally effect outcomes. The best thoughts to think are those that help you feel joy.

* **Power of Unconditional Love:** Unconditional love is the strongest power there is and is most often used to support others.

* **Power of Energy:** We are all energetically connected. Every action has energy. Every individual should be conscious of this, for their actions always impact themselves and others. Choose your thoughts, words and actions wisely, for they can permanently impact your destiny or another's.

* **Power to Influence:** Every interaction you have with others influences your life and theirs. Choose your words and actions wisely.

* **Power of Conscious Creation:** All answers are inside each person. Key components to your ability to consciously create include watching your thoughts and eliminating emotional contradictions which are not in congruence with your values. Don't look to others for answers, for their energy

can interfere with yours. Your moto should be, "Don't go out, go in." When all is in congruence such as thoughts, emotions, values, actions, etc., your true, balanced beauty emerges.

POWER TOOLS

- **Power of Cleaning and Clearing:** Reevaluate your relationships to identify disharmonies with your values and goals. Remove any objects that have emotional attachments of hurt associated with them. Clean up any areas of clutter as these also distract the mind. Eliminating negative visual cues allows your mind to easily focus on things positively.

- **Power of Imagination:** Imagining needs to be practiced with care. Choose thoughts, words and outcomes carefully because, ultimately, what you think and feel, you create.

3 CROSSING THE THRESHOLD

Totsy moved to what would be her last foster home. It was the home of another aunt who had re-married a rich farmer. In fact, Aunt Evie had divorced her first husband to marry Samuel Ordel Blackmore.

Divorce was quite rare in the U.S. in those days, but Samuel was a big talker and chased her endlessly. All his sweet talking fueled the dissolution of her aunt's first marriage. He filled Aunt Evie's mind with images of an easy life and all the nice things she would have being married to a rich farmer.

In reality, behind closed doors, Samuel was a much different person. He may have had lots of money and a big farm, but his big heart was only giving when it was on his terms. He also concealed a very dark side of himself which her aunt only discovered after they were married.

Although Totsy was acquainted with her cousins, she had no idea of the cruel, repressed family life they lived, under the control of Uncle Samuel. There were family secrets not privy to outsiders, although outsiders could surmise due to his occasional public displays of alarming anger. Once there, Totsy became the new punching bag victim of choice by the vile farmer, although he would take turns and periodically beat his son as well. Even his brothers feared him.

When town folk saw him, they scattered, not wanting to engage in any sort of conversation with him for fear it would set him off and result in a fierce beating. His presence flip-flopped between radiating extreme happiness when there was something he wanted, to emitting extreme anger if he didn't get his way. His eyes bore hatred and disgust for others if he held contempt for them.

The slightest thing could set him off, like not putting away a shovel, the hay bales stacked crooked or a car cutting him off in traffic. He would begin by verbally abusing the person, saying they were good for nothing and that they would never amount to anything. He would then launch into slapping and pushing them around. If they fell down, he kicked them.

But with Totsy and his only son John, he was always careful to only kick and hit them in the trunk of their bodies so that the bruising would be covered up by their clothes. His favorite way of berating them was to say they were "nothing but two-bit…"

Cousin John and Totsy became close. Since John was already wary of his father's moods, he took Totsy under his wing. He showed her how to pull the cutter with Old Mike and how to drive a tractor.

Old Mike was a big, all-white gentle horse. He was Totsy's favorite animal on the farm. He would pucker his lips and blow between them when he wanted something special to eat like an apple, carrot or some corn. Sometimes he nuzzled under her arms for affection.

Young Totsy usually drove the tractor so John could be the one to load the bales of hay in the flat wagon at harvest time. As she grew older and stronger, they took turns at slinging the bales onto the flat wagon or stacking the bales in the barn loft.

After another exhausting day, Totsy laid in bed listening to the leaves in the trees as they danced in the chilly, gusty, autumn wind outside her bedroom window. Cool air blew in through the cracks around the windows causing the shades and curtains to bellow out like balloon shapes. Before falling asleep, she silently deliberated her future; a life of her own, a life full of love and happiness.

She pulled the patchwork quilt up over her ears as she turned on her side. She knew life wasn't meant to be like this, as she was experiencing right now, with this bully foster parent, Uncle Samuel. She had already experienced a loving home with parents who were kind, loving and giving with siblings who looked out for each other. She longed for this kind of life again.

She wrestled with her feelings of anger for being tossed around from foster family to foster family and feelings of jealousy that her two younger step-sisters were placed in a better stable home. She felt angry with her mother and biological father for having her out of wed-lock and putting the illegitimate- bastard child label upon her.

At such a young age, she understood the cruelty of life and what people can inflict on others. The horrors of World War II were a daily reminder of man's brutality against other human life. The Germans had been bombing London for some time and Japan had just bombed Pearl Harbor throwing the U.S. into the war. She heard President Roosevelt give his Day of Infamy speech on the radio which rallied congress and gained support for the war effort. Unbeknownst to her, President Roosevelt routinely put aside any physical limitations he was experiencing with his polio by strapping on leg braces which helped him to portray a brave, strong leader to the U.S. citizens and Congress.

Unknowingly, Totsy had followed President Roosevelt's example in that she attempted to counteract sad feelings by buying presents for her younger cousin, Helen, such as socks at Christmas or candy at Easter. She was projecting a loving, giving demeanor but deep inside, she wished someone was thinking of her in this way.

With the war, many men were enlisting into the Armed Forces, and this caused a shortage of workers. Totsy and several of her schoolmates were hired to work at the local egg plant for a few hours after school each day. Some of the eggs were dehydrated and shipped overseas to feed the military personnel. In fact, there were soldiers who oversaw the whole operation in the plant. Totsy would see Bobby Schmidt occasionally talking to the military men.

At the plant, Totsy saw her previous foster parent, Mr. Dee once again. His limp made him ineligible for military service. The last couple years living at Aunt Evie's and Uncle Samuel's farm gave her a new perspective on her time with Mr. Dee and his family. They accepted her as she was and never bothered her. It had been easy living with his family when compared to the abuse and beatings she was enduring at the farm.

Totsy and the other schoolgirls were candlers on the line, while Bobby and other boys were boxers. With their mid-teenage years, Bobby was starting to come around and be nice to Totsy. She often gave him a ride home so he wouldn't have to hop the train.

She discovered during these drives, that he had a tough life, just like her. She already knew his father was German and his mother was Irish which when their tough and stubborn personalities were combined with a little bit of liquor, an explosion of anger was bound to happen.

Bobby shared that his parents both immigrated to the U.S. after World War I and met in Milwaukee. Like several other European immigrants, his parents were drawn to Merylville for the rich farmland. His parents both thought they had put behind the horrors of war when they left their respective countries. But the stress of the second war combined with the economic downturn of the Great Depression weighed heavily on them. Plus they worried about all the family they left behind in their respective homelands. Occasional letters from Ireland were still arriving but there were no longer any from Germany.

Bobby proudly shared how he was planning to enlist in the Army. His father had taught him German and he thought his fluency in the language would be of value once he enlisted. The military was going to offer him the opportunity for a better life than what he was experiencing at his miserable home.

The one thing Totsy liked best about working at the egg plant was that it took her into town on a regular basis. To her delight, she and Jade were occasionally able to see each other whether passing by each other on the street or when they specifically arranged time to visit. Sometimes, Jade popped in at the egg plant with something special for Totsy and the others to eat such as a cake or biscuits.

After an especially nasty beating, Totsy experienced pain in her abdomen. It persisted for a few days. Then one day, while working at the egg plant, she collapsed to the floor in pain. Her aunt and uncle were called to take her to the hospital. It was appendicitis.

During the examination, the doctor and Catholic nun nurses saw the bruising on Totsy's torso. When asked about it, she declined to share any details. They pitied her predicament, knowing that it was a member of her foster home that was causing the harm. With no further information, they could not help her plus they surmised for them to get involved might cause Totsy more harm than good.

The hospital staff was nice and supportive of her during her stay. Even the cleaning lady took time to make sure she was comfortable. She knew Totsy's mother and remembered when she was in the hospital after the house fire. She showed Totsy her mother's hospital room. Totsy studied the room for a moment and thought about how her mother struggled with her severe burns, knowing that she was leaving behind three young children. The experience was a little eerie to Totsy, but she was glad to have seen the room.

During Totsy's hospitalization, some of her school mates came to visit her as did her Aunt Evie and Cousin Helen. Rae came up every day after school to spend time with her. One day she shared the news that she had accepted a teaching position in California. Even Bobby Schmidt visited her once. He had a black eye which he claimed was caused by running into a cabinet door at home. Totsy knew better. He shared with her how he heard some guys were lying about their ages and enlisting early. She read between the lines and knew Bobby was planning on doing the same.

Her dear old friend Jade had heard of her condition and paid her a visit too. Totsy perked up at the sight of Jade and threw her arms out to embrace her, feeling the fragility in her aging body.

"My dear, how are you feeling?" Jade inquired.

"Much better," Totsy replied with a smile on her face. "And you?" Totsy asked as she cradled Jade's hand in hers.

Jade brushed back the curls on Totsy's face, taking in how she had matured over the last few years. Totsy was now sixteen years old.

"Oh, I am doing just fine child. The church has me hopping with all the Red Cross troop packages we are helping to put together."

For once, she and Jade could talk freely, but did so ever discretely.

"I know your foster home life hasn't been all that accommodating. I'm sorry dear that I am too old to take you in."

"That's alright. I know, Jade." Totsy patted the top of her hand to comfort Jade.

"Have you thought about what you will do Totsy? Soon you will be old enough to be on your own."

Totsy crooked her finger and waved Jade to come in closer.

She whispered, "I haven't told anyone, but my friend Rae invited me to California. She got a job as a school teacher out there. I've been secretly saving some of my egg plant money for some time to help get me out on my own. I have a few more months to go. You know I have to pay them rent for living on the farm. Plus they get the $3 a month from the county too."

Jade stretched out her arms again, and they hugged.

"Then I guess the gift I bought for you is so very appropriate." Jade handed Totsy her book on the Kings and Queens of Europe. You will need something to read on that long train ride."

Jade showed her the inscription she wrote which Totsy read out loud, "To Elizabeth Rose, do what is right for you. Listen to yourself, your heart and your desires. Love, Jade."

Every payday, Totsy cashed her egg plant check and paid her weekly rent to Uncle Samuel. She put some of her paycheck in the bank but unbeknownst to Uncle Samuel, Aunt Evie and Cousin Helen, she was keeping some of her payday cash and hiding it in her bedroom window roll-up blind. This was her stash of money that would buy her train ticket and cover her trip to California. Each night, Totsy would count the money to make sure it was all there. She almost had enough money for the ticket, but needed extra cash to live on once she arrived and was able to find work. She was a little upset with herself for spending $16 on a permanent wave, but that was before Rae invited her to California.

Before falling asleep each night, Totsy laid in bed thinking about the life she was going to create for herself. She remembered Grandma Friedrich's and Jade's words that the power was in her heart, inside her. She knew the way she was treated on the farm by Uncle Samuel wasn't right, that it wasn't a nurturing environment. She had experienced unconditional love when her mother was alive and when she lived with Grandma and Grandpa Friedrich. She knew that there was a better life for her out there and that one day, she would have a loving family of her own. It became her nightly ritual to envision all the steps on the way to seeing her friend Rae and creating a new, better life for herself in California.

World War II was in full swing with the Allies planning the Normandy Invasion. Great Britain was hunkered down due to getting bombed from the Germans. The U.S. citizens were on pins and needles, worried that their U.K. ally would be invaded and that the U.S. would be next. Troops were being deployed to the Philippines and New Guinea. Gas was being rationed and all new car production was halted to divert the steel and other raw materials to the war effort. More women were going to work in factories with all the men being deployed.

Tensions ran high on the farm as Cousin John would soon be off to war. One late afternoon, Uncle Samuel came in to the house looking for someone to bully. Totsy was helping her aunt prepare dinner by peeling potatoes at the kitchen sink and this was the day that Totsy had enough. Uncle Samuel had been drinking at the local watering hole and was in a foul mood. He found Totsy in the kitchen, getting dinner ready with Aunt Evie. He started by pushing her from behind, smacking her on the back of the head and calling her a "good for nothing." Then he picked up some of the potato skins and accused her of cutting too much skin off the potatoes.

The pushing and punching started, but after a few rounds, Totsy found the courage to fight back. All those hay bales she had flung into the back of the wagon and up into the barn loft had built up her upper body strength and her confidence. With him being slightly tipsy, she saw her chance to push him back. He fell against the kitchen table. Aunt Evie called out to both of them, "Calm down!" She tried to tell Uncle Samuel to go and sleep it off, but Uncle Samuel was fiery mad. He grabbed the paring knife Totsy had used to peel the potatoes and lunged at her.

Cousin John was just coming in when he heard the commotion. He grabbed Uncle Samuel from behind, putting him in a choke hold and slamming him up against the wall. The impact caused a split in Uncle Samuel's upper lip. Cousin John grabbed a fistful of Uncle Samuel's hair, pulled his head back and shared a few choice words with him. Uncle Samuel understood. He was no longer the strong brute in the household. The hard farm work he imposed upon Totsy and John had made them both physically stronger than him.

Defeated, he exited the kitchen for the front porch to rock away his drink while they continued to prepare the evening meal. With the end of the school year coming near, Cousin John would leave for the Army soon, and Totsy feared things would only get worse. The whole event reinforced her decision to leave for California.

POWERISMS

🌸 **Power of Dreams:** Achieving dreams requires plotting and planning. Words, thoughts and imagination play an important role and must be chosen wisely.

🌸 **Power of Self-Respect:** It's a form of self-love, self-belief and self-worth. By not imposing boundaries in how others treat you, you invite a lack of respect. Have empathy for others but don't allow others to take advantage of you.

🌸 **Power of Time:** Time allows one to see a different perspective which can lead to life-changing decisions.

🌸 **Abuse of Power:** Power when abused is the exertion of unnecessary control or manipulation of other individuals for one's own personal gain. The ego is usually involved and eventually these actions by the abuser sets them back from anything they thought they gained by their controlling, manipulative actions.

POWER TOOLS

🔨 **Expressing One's Self:** Take time to express your feelings along with your desired new outcome when you are repeatedly experiencing frustrating situations.

🔨 **Making Decisions:** When decisions are made, this sets in motion other events in one's life.

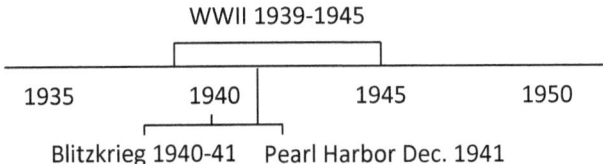

WWII 1939-1945

| 1935 | 1940 | 1945 | 1950 |

Blitzkrieg 1940-41   Pearl Harbor Dec. 1941

4 EL CAPTAIN

Totsy hustled to the train station with her hard-cover suitcase in hand. She had been dreaming of this day for so long. It all seemed so surreal. The stationmaster greeted her with a smile, "Hello Totsy."

"Elizabeth Rose," she stood tall as she corrected him, "Hi, Mr. Weston."

She was looking rather stylish in her skirt suit and fascinator feather hat as she opened up her purse and handed him the money for the fare.

"One ticket to Chicago please."

"Alright," he said as he swept the money toward him with one hand then flipped a ticket on the counter for her. "Here you go. Going to visit some friends are you?"

"No, family," she replied. She lied, not wanting Uncle Samuel or Aunt Evie to find out the truth of where she was going.

"Well, have a fun trip. The train should be here," but before he could finish his sentence, the train whistle could be heard off in the distance. He smiled as he finished the last words, "Any minute. The south bound platform awaits you my dear."

"Thank you, Mr. Weston."

Elizabeth Rose picked up her ticket and stuck it in her coat pocket. She slowly strode to the south side platform with her suitcase and satchel in hand. She looked to see if she recognized any of the other travelers and to her relief there were only people she recognized but didn't really know.

CHUG A LUG, CHUG A LUG, CHUG A LUG the steam engine train went as it slowly glided into the station. Elizabeth Rose stood off to the side and behind some other people to shelter herself in case anyone got off the train that she knew. She didn't want to have to answer any last minute questions before boarding the train. A few passengers exited the train before the conductor gave the "All Aboard" call for the waiting passengers to board. Elizabeth Rose scampered on to the last train car, slid her suitcase on the luggage rack, and found an open window-seat.

With a call of the whistle, the train lurched forward as it started to exit the station. Elizabeth Rose slouched in her seat in an attempt to hide herself so as to not be seen by anyone who would tell of her escape. The steam engine train started out going chooga chooga chooga, chooga chooga chooga then switched over to CHUGGA chugga chugga CHUGGA chugga chugga as it got more power then let out a CHOO CHOOOOOOO! Once it fully ramped up to full speed Elizabeth Rose turned back for one last look of Merylville. The further out of town the train got, the more excited anticipation enveloped her.

Her eyes were wide open as she took in the

scenery that ran along the tracks. She had never been this far south of Merylville. She adjusted herself in her seat as she settled into the gentle sway of the train cars gliding along the tracks. At this point it was all farm fields to look at that would change from pasture fields with grazing cows to neatly planted fields of wheat, potatoes or cabbage.

Soon Elizabeth Rose settled into her seat, still clutching her purse on her lap with her satchel at her feet. She propped her head up against the window as the excitement and stress from the execution of all her plotting and planning seemed to leave her body. She was free.

This was a big day. She was moving forward in creating a new life for herself. She was no longer being a hired slave to foster farmers nor beat up and pushed around by Uncle Samuel anymore. She briefly wondered what they would do with her gone and Cousin John going off to war soon.

With the morning sun warming up the train car, Elizabeth Rose found herself feeling sleepy. She still had approximately three and a half hours until she passed through Milwaukee then another two until she disembarked in Chicago. She stared blankly at the tick of the telephone poles that the train passed by before giving into her heavy eyelids for a quick nap, dreaming of what she would see when she got closer to those two cities.

The trip seemed to be taking forever due to all the small town train stations they stopped at en route to Milwaukee. The train cars were filling up too. Feeling a little shy and fidgety, Elizabeth Rose just kept to herself as the people shuffled on and off the train. She attempted to read Jade's book, but found it hard to concentrate, using it as a ploy to discourage interaction from the other passengers.

Soon with the continual chug of the train, she noticed the approaching skyline change. The fields were replaced with houses upon houses that changed into buildings upon buildings and finally she was in the heart of the city of Milwaukee. Her eyes were amazed at the tall office buildings and the stone facades that finished them. They had brick buildings in Merylville but not as tall as these.

People in her train car started to gather up their things to make their exit, as Elizabeth Rose sat mesmerized by the hustle and bustle in the terminal. It was here she had to make a train change. She nimbly grabbed her suitcase off the rack with her satchel over her shoulder and purse in hand. She noticed a lot more service men milling about the crowd. A few Army and Marine service men dotted the crowd but the station was mostly filled with Navy sailors.

As she scooted to the next platform, she noticed the war posters encouraging the purchase of Victory Bonds, joining the military or encouraging women to work for the war effort. She heard the cries of a newspaper boy barking out the headlines to entice buyers and saw a vendor with a queue of people ready to purchase candy and food. A diner in the station had people lingering about their lunch plates or grabbing one last sip of coffee before they exited to catch a train.

Soon she was swept up in the wave of passengers all making their way to their destinations. She easily saw the signs for the Chicago platform and she was in luck for the train was waiting. She confirmed with the conductor that it was the right train before entering a car. Only a man and a woman were onboard as she found herself a seat. There was a sense of an eerie silence and calm inside the train car compared to the noise from the people and trains at the station. Then out of nowhere came a swarm of sailors, all wearing their dress whites. The quiet in the train car was soon broken by the noise of the bunch as they gathered around and began to board. Soon Elizabeth Rose was surrounded by the seaman recruits who took note of her stylish demeanor and they began to volley for seats close to her.

"Hi young lady, these seats open?" asked one of the brave sailors.

She shook her head 'yes' and they soon piled in around her. She was a little embarrassed by all the attention.

"Now where would a pretty young thing like you be off to, traveling all by yourself?"

"Chicago" Elizabeth Rose replied, as she nervously played with her necklace from Jade.

"Oh, fancy meeting you on this train. You got yourself a fella down there you're going to see?"

The other sailors started to jab and jeer at his bold inquiry, "Cutting to the chase McEvoy, aren't you?" Another shouted, "You go man!"

Elizabeth Rose was taken back by all the attention and boldly stated, "I don't think it's any of your business why I am going to Chicago."

The crowd of sailors let out an "Ooh" more to tease McEvoy. Others chimed in "Now you did it." And "Now you put her off."

"Easy fella's," McEvoy retorted. "Just trying to get to know the lady."

Some buddies taunted McEvoy, "Uh huh", "Sure McEvoy."

"Show her your tattoos," one sailor from behind them called out. The guys started to laugh. McEvoy gave them all a look to let them know they were ruining it for him.

He leaned over and showed her the boat anchor he had tattooed on his inside forearm.

"You see this? I had this done to commemorate going into the Navy."

From behind, a sailor shouted, "Not that one. The one where you had Susan tattooed on your shoulder."

The guys broke out into hysterical laughter. McEvoy recovered by saying, "Don't mind them. They're just jealous"

Elizabeth Rose just took it all in. She remembered how at school Bobby would try to get her attention and she took this all in stride.

"So what's your name Beautiful?" he asked.

They settled into a nice conversation in which he shared he was getting off at the Naval Station Great Lakes. As the train neared his station he bid her farewell and safe travels to Chicago.

Another passenger hastily took McEvoy's seat but kept to himself, engrossed in reading the newspaper. Elizabeth Rose mainly directed her attention to the scenery outside and contemplated her future. The train speed began to slow down as more houses were sprouting up along the train tracks. The conductor was blowing his whistle much more often at the road crossings, the closer they got into the city of Chicago. From a distance, she could see the magnificent skyline filled with city skyscrapers.

As the train entered the heart of the city, Elizabeth

Rose was intrigued by the three flats with the balconies out back and she occasionally saw women hanging their laundry. Water towers dotted the roof tops of the apartment buildings and electrical and phone wires hung from poles to the buildings. She was amazed at how much concrete there was along with the number of cars and buses, and the amount of people moving about the streets. She wondered if any of those cars were some of the notorious gangsters that were written about in the newspapers and talked about on the radio.

Occasionally, she saw trolley cars riding rails in the streets and what must have been a subway train on elevated tracks. Then the train with slow chugging movements eked its way into the vast openness of the station railyard. With each passing moment of her journey, she was being exposed to things she had only seen pictures of and read brief captions in magazines or newspapers or saw in the movies. It was all real but seemed strange to see in real life to Elizabeth Rose.

Again, Elizabeth Rose was shuffled along with the wave of travelers into Chicago's Grand Central Station. Once she passed through the doors, the vast openness of the station enveloped her vision. She was stunned to see such a large enclosed area with the vaulted ceiling rising up on steel arches and the polished marble floors.

The ticketing line was long but moved quickly. Elizabeth Rose paid her $40 fare and was directed to the beautiful waiting room of the station. She found a rest room on the way and also purchased a sandwich and bottle of cola from a deli located in the terminal.

Finding a seat against the wall in the waiting room, she devoured her sandwich in no time. From this vantage point, she could see the clock on the wall to watch the time. She had a view of the whole waiting area in which to people watch. The interior was exquisitely decorated with stained glass windows, Corinthian columns along with high polished marble floors and a fireplace. She had never seen such opulence before and thought this must be how the rich and royals live.

With anxiety building inside her, she stood up and paced about, back and forth, and flapped her ticket in her hand. All she wanted was to get on the train and be on her way to California. She watched the hand movements of the clock tick off each second of every minute.

At exactly 15 minutes to boarding time, she picked up her suitcase and satchel then found her way to the boarding gate. People were jammed up waiting to be let through to the boarding platform gates. Elizabeth Rose found a spot against the wall. It helped her from getting pushed and shoved around as, more and more people filled the boarding gate area like sardines. The cramped, warm area triggered a bout of claustrophobia in her.

Finally, people were being let in. Elizabeth Rose quickly found a place in the swiftly moving line. Once her ticket was punched and she had passed through the gate, she quickened her pace to get on the train. Glancing up she caught a glimpse of the famous train and it made her smile. There it stood in all its glory: the El Captain locomotive wearing her yellow and red war bonnet in honor of the Allied Troops fighting in the war.

Excitement filled Elizabeth Rose with each step she took toward the El Captain. She easily got swept up in the sardine packed crowd that opened up slightly as the people started to embark the train. Once settled onboard, relief overcame Elizabeth Rose as she reclined back in her seat. She pulled her hat off as the other passengers settled in around her.

A woman a little older than her approached. In a high pitched voice, she introduced herself, "Hi, I'm Catherine. Mind if I take this seat?"

"Hi, I'm Elizabeth Rose. Be my guest." She smiled back.

"You heading to Los Angeles?" Catherine asked as she put her bag under the seat in front of her.

Elizabeth Rose reached for her satchel to place her hat on it, "Yes. And you?"

Catherine pulled her gloves off and placed them in her purse, "Yeah, my agent is sending me to audition out there. Have you ever been there?"

"No, have you?"

"Just one other time, for another audition. I didn't get that part. It's a long trip, but" Catherine pushed a button to recline the seat back, "at least we can catch some sleep."

Catherine took the pins out of her hat and then pushed it over her forehead to block the light from hitting her eyes. From under the make-shift visor she continued, "I always like all the handsome soldiers I see on these trips." She released her inclined seat and sprang up to a sitting position. Her hat landed in her lap.

"You have a beau?"

"No" Elizabeth Rose replied as she shook her head.

"I do." Catherine gleefully showed her engagement ring and quickly snapped open her purse to show

Elizabeth Rose a photograph. "We went to school together. This was taken last Christmas. When he comes back, we're getting married."

"That's wonderful. You must be excited."

"Yeah, I can't wait. He's over in England right now. At least I think he still is with the Normandy invasion just starting." Catherine reached into her purse again. Elizabeth Rose's stomach sank a little bit for Catherine. On D-Day alone there were thousands that died and with each passing day the casualties continued to climb. "Here's the last letter I got from him." Catherine opened it up for Elizabeth Rose to see and started to read it to her. It was as if Catherine was looking for reassurance that he was alright and returning home to her.

"I'm sure he is just fine. How are the plans coming?"

Confidently Catherine told her, "I got everything all done. The church, the banquet hall, the invitations are picked out and my dress." With a bubbly giggle she added, "I just need my groom."

The "ALL ABORAD' last call was heard in the background and the final boarding whistle blew. The diesel engine was ramping up along with the repetitive CLANG, CLANG, CLANG of the bell that could be heard followed by a lurch forward once the El Captain set in motion. The two women made small talk as the excitement of the windy city was being left behind. Office buildings flowed into manufacturing buildings that flowed into backyard views of the flats that lined the city streets, and followed the tracks out of the city. Soon it was once again open, flat, farmland that filled the view for miles and miles.

It was nearing dusk when Catherine's stomach

rumbled. "Say, why don't you join me in getting something to eat at the snack lounge?"

Elizabeth Rose agreed and the two women made their way to the lounge car. The ruckus in the lounge could be heard before they even opened the carriage door. It became instantly silent as the two of them entered. It was mostly full of service men that turned all their eyes toward them. And as quickly as the silence ensued, the conversations re-erupted around them.

With a devilish grin on her face, Catherine tapped Elizabeth Rose's arm as they approached the counter, "Hey, maybe we'll find you a man on this trip. Lots of cute soldier boys in here."

Elizabeth Rose was slightly embarrassed at her comment.

"I'll have a Tom Collins please. Honey, would you like anything to drink?"

"I'll just have a Coca-Cola," Elizabeth Rose requested.

Concerned, Catherine inquired, "Honey, don't you drink?"

"I saw my Uncle Samuel drink enough, but I do partake every now and then. We always had a keg of beer on the farm and homemade wine. My stomach is just a little upset right now."

"I understand. Let's get some food in you."

They placed their orders to go and sipped their drinks while they waited for their sandwiches.

Gazing around the room, Catherine suddenly blurted out, "Elizabeth, I think he likes you."

Surprised, Elizabeth Rose asked "Who?"

"Well, don't look now. He'll know we're talking about him. That soldier over there with the dark hair.

He's cute. He's got wings above his pocket."

After a few seconds Catherine said, "Ok, now look."

Elizabeth Rose turned his way. Just as she looked, he lifted his head and turned her way; their eyes met. She smiled at him and he smiled back. The brief exchange only lasted a second, but seemed to be frozen in time for Elizabeth Rose.

Catherine slapped Elizabeth Rose's arm, "See, it was kismet. You were meant to be on this train." With schoolgirl glee Catherine let out, "I'm so happy for you." Then she suddenly straightened up.

The young soldier approached Elizabeth Rose from behind. "Excuse me. But can I buy you a drink?" he asked her.

Elizabeth Rose turned and instantly became weak in her knees. She turned around to find him standing right next to her. He glanced down into her blue eyes. She smiled gently and shyly blurted out, "Sure."

The soldier nodded toward the attendant who set up another cola for her.

Catherine spoke up, "Where you heading to soldier?"

"California. And you two ladies?"

"Both Los Angeles" Catherine replied. Picking up her drink, she shared with a smirk on her face, "I'll leave you two to talk." Catherine moved to a nearby table of soldiers and began flirty chit-chat with the men.

He held his hand out to introduce himself, "My name is Tom."

"Elizabeth Rose" she shared as she shook his hand.

"What's taking you on this journey to Los

Angeles?"

"My friend got a job as a teacher out there and invited me to stay with her until I get settled. And you?"

"I'm heading to the Santa Ana Army Air Base. From there I'll be deployed overseas."

Their conversation barely got started when their to-go orders arrived. Catherine made her way back over to Elizabeth Rose.

"Well, soldier boy," Catherine injected as she quickly set her drink glass on the lounge bar. "We have to go eat but maybe you can find us a little later. We're a couple cars back from here."

Elizabeth Rose was unsure of what was going on as Catherine picked up the sandwiches. She stammered out "I will see you?" to which Tom replied with a big smile "You bet."

Catherine grabbed Elizabeth Rose by her arm to escort her out. Elizabeth Rose turned for one last look and gave a smile to Tom who was watching them leave.

Once the train car door closed and they were making their way up the aisle, Elizabeth Rose asked what was going on.

"I didn't want you to get too chatty with him. You want him to want to chase you. He'll find you. Just you wait and see."

With full belly's, sleep easily overtook Elizabeth Rose and Catherine. Until one of the after midnight train stops in which the train abruptly jerked. Catherine only stirred in her seat while Elizabeth Rose was startled wide awake for a while. She gazed out into the darkness of the night, still able to see the tick of the telephone poles gliding by under the light of the moon. She wondered if anyone back home was looking for her yet. Surely, Aunt Evie and Uncle Samuel had to be wondering where she was, but yet she didn't care. She was putting behind her all the abuse she endured for the last ten to twelve years of her life with them and the other foster families.

Elizabeth Rose realized she had come a long way. Not only traveling from Merylville, Wisconsin but also in her journey of life. She thought about her mother and wondered how she would feel about her taking this long trip to California by herself. Her thoughts shifted to Jade and how she was such a godsend to her. She would miss her most and was sad about leaving her behind. Once she got settled she was going to ring her up to tell her of her trip and whereabouts. Next, she wondered how both Cousin John and her school mate Bobby were doing too.

Elizabeth Rose managed to drift off to sleep, once again, until the bright morning sunlight peeked in. People had begun to move about the train, making sleep almost impossible, plus a bathroom break was much needed by both Elizabeth Rose and Catherine.

Elizabeth Rose was just fixing her makeup when Tom found his way to her. In the morning light, his green eyes exploded off his dark, olive green Army jacket which contrasted with his dark brown hair. He invited her for morning coffee in the lounge car, which with a nod of permission and a wink from Catherine, she eagerly joined him.

Tom was ever the polite gentleman with her, opening the doors and pulling out her chair to seat her. He proudly introduced her to his Army mates who were sincere and pleased to meet her. Some of them were bombardiers, gunners, or navigators serving in the U.S. Army Air Corps and trained on the flying fortress: the B-17.

Elizabeth Rose was at ease with him and she enjoyed their conversation as they learned more about each other. He was trained as a B-17 bomber pilot at Santa Anna. His brief visit home was after he completed his flight training and now he was heading back to deploy to Europe.

He was first generation born to Polish immigrants who migrated to the U.S. after World War I. The stress of this latest war took its toll on his family in that they lost all contact with their relatives back home. His father's parting words to him when he left Chicago was "Go get those S.O.B.'s."

The train was now traveling through Trinidad, Colorado and the mountains were starting to come into close view. Tom could see the awe in her eyes as she studied the mountain ranges from afar and in particular at the flatness of Fishers Peak. She shared how she worked in the egg plant and also worked at the foster farms. He saw immense strength in her for all she had been through. With the coffee gone and donuts eaten, their conversation came to a standstill. Elizabeth Rose thanked him for breakfast and stated that she should be getting back to Catherine. Tom escorted her back to her train car.

Glancing up into his eyes she asked, "Will I see you again?"

With a smile he replied, "Why, yes, I will come by later if that is ok with you?"

"That would be great" she confirmed and he reached down to kiss her gently on her cheek.

Catherine was all astir at the sight of all this, demanding to know every detail once Elizabeth Rose was settled back in her seat. "See I told you. You did just fine by coming back when you did."

Tom sought out Elizabeth Rose at about seven-thirty that evening. He invited Catherine to join them in the lounge car. Some country western singers had boarded the train and were in the lounge with their guitars, tambourines and harmonicas playing for drinks. All the passengers were jovial, joining in to sing when they knew the tunes. Catherine was busy being the onboard starlet and innocently flirting with the enlisted men.

A warm sunset blanketed the lounge car right before dusk settled in. The sun played off Elizabeth Rose's and Tom's faces as they sat at a corner table. He reached out to hold her hand in his as they watched the sun disappear behind the curves of the winding Grand Canyon Arizona Mountains. They were smitten with each other and he talked about how he wanted to stay in contact with her.

By midnight, the crowd was thinning out and most had gone to retire for the night. Elizabeth Rose shared her first kiss with Tom by the lounge car door. He walked her back to her seat and bid her to sleep well. Elizabeth Rose was overwhelmed with all the new romance emotions she was feeling. She felt light-headed and giddy on top of all the anticipatory anxiety she was feeling with her move to California.

The clear light of the day, and sunny blue skies greeted Elizabeth Rose as she awoke from her light slumber. She barely slept a wink with all the excitement she was feeling and all the passengers shuffling about the car from time to time. Tom checked in with her after the 6am San Bernardino stop, to let her know he arranged for a porter to help her and Catherine with their bags. He asked her to wait at the platform to meet him and the porter so he could walk her out to the station.

"See girly," Catherine slugged Elizabeth Rose in the arm, "I told you he liked you. He's a keeper. I'm so happy for you. Let's keep in touch."

The two women exchanged addresses then they settled down, taking in the scrubby, desert scenery which changed between orange, lime and lemon orchards, potato fields, and small towns sprinkled with palm trees.

Once the Pasadena stop was made, it was a short half hour train ride to Union Passenger Station in Los Angeles. The train couldn't get there fast enough as the excitement continued to build in Elizabeth Rose. On one hand she didn't want to depart from Tom, and on the other hand she was so excited to see her friend Rae. She started to drum her fingers on her chair arm, as if it would speed up the train. The conductor made his sweep through the car to check tickets and offer any passenger assistance. Once the El Captain rolled into the wide rail staging area of the railyard, the push was on by the passengers to get organized for their disembarkment from the train.

Tom and the porter found Elizabeth Rose and Catherine patiently waiting on the platform. Elizabeth Rose felt slightly awkward and under duress as they walked up to the station. Her mind was racing for she didn't know how to handle parting ways with Tom and meeting up with her friend Rae.

Once inside the station, Catherine thanked Tom for assisting with her bag.

"Keep in touch, girly" Catherine commanded as she gave Elizabeth Rose a hug goodbye.

With a wink Catherine added, "I want to be invited to the wedding."

Camera flashes started to go off as a group of reporters were swarming a man in the distance. Catherine squealed at the anticipation of finding out who the celebrity star was and grabbed her bag to dash off. She turned back with a wave of her hand, and bid the two new lovebird's adieu.

POWERISIMS

❋ **Power of an Open Heart:** Sometimes your desires are presented to you in a slightly different format and the challenge will be to recognize and accept that which is presented to you as fulfilling that desire, that goal. An open heart is flexible and accepting.

❋ **Power of Going with the Flow:** Sometimes positive outcomes can happen just with going with the flow of life. Other times, if no conscious effort is put into life events, it can leave one feeling as a victim of circumstances.

POWER TOOLS

✎ **Power of Action:** Desire (motivation and emotion) propels an individual into action. Once a decision is made, your action is the steps taken to achieve a goal which is supported by a value. Action sets in motion change, and sets an individual on a new path.

✎ **Power of Risks:** Sometimes caution must be thrown to the wind and action taken to propel you on your way to achieving a desired outcome.

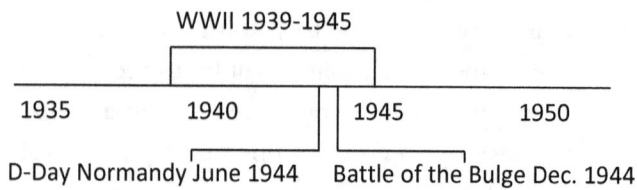

WWII 1939-1945

| 1935 | 1940 | 1945 | 1950 |

D-Day Normandy June 1944   Battle of the Bulge Dec. 1944

5 BELLY OF THE WHALE

The commotion of the reporters surrounding actor Humphrey Bogart created a diversion, so Elizabeth Rose and Tom could have one last kiss. They were saying their goodbyes when Elizabeth Rose's friend, Rae, found them.

Rae enthusiastically greeted Elizabeth Rose, "You made it!" and the two of them hugged. "Who's your friend?" she inquired with a smile and an outstretched hand.

Tom confidently shook her hand, "You must be Rae. I'm Tom. Tom Krol. My buddies tell me Tommy Dorsey opened his own place called Casino Gardens. I would really like Elizabeth Rose to come this weekend. Will you join her and maybe bring some of your single friends along?"

Rae saw some of Tom's Army buddies gather up behind him and she happily agreed. The men escorted the two ladies out to the taxis. Fresh morning sunshine greeted Elizabeth Rose's face welcoming her to the fresh start she was just beginning for her life.

During the short ride to Rae's place, Elizabeth Rose was impressed with the Spanish architecture predominate in the area and the oil pumpjacks and wells that dotted the greater Los Angeles community. She found Rae's apartment very accommodating for a guest. The first thing she did was to ring Jade and let her know she arrived safely to Rae's place. After lunch, Rae then gave Elizabeth Rose a tour of the neighborhood during which they grocery shopped. That evening, they ate a celebratory dinner, at a small Italian restaurant, and upon returning back to Rae's house, Elizabeth Rose turned in early. She was exhausted from all the adventures she encountered on her solo trip to California.

All bright-eyed the next morning, Elizabeth Rose immediately began her work search. She easily maneuvered the bus routes and found her way about town. She found herself distracted with thoughts of Tom throughout the day. Wondering how his deployment plans were going and looking forward to seeing him on Saturday. With a smile she thought to herself, "So, this is what being in love is like."

Saturday couldn't get there soon enough. Rae and Elizabeth Rose helped each other do their hair for the dance that evening. Tom was waiting for Elizabeth Rose at the Casino Garden's main door. He had a big smile on his face as he greeted the two ladies and paid for their admission. A couple of Rae's new school teacher friends were already there.

The dance hall was hopping with all sorts of people milling about and packed on the dance floor. Tom took Elizabeth Rose by the arm to walk her and Rae over to his military buddies. He complimented Elizabeth Rose on how pretty she looked in her blue floral frock dress. Proudly, he introduced them to his table of friends who were waiting to meet them. Frank was instantly drawn to Rae and immediately asked her to dance.

Elizabeth Rose made idle conversation with people at the table. One of Tom's buddies had a girl with him named Sally. She shouted out over the music to Elizabeth Rose, "Come – have a seat over here" as she motioned toward the open chair.

Sally began to immediately chat with her. She shared that she was a waitress at an elite, Hollywood, country club. Sally asked what Elizabeth Rose did for a living. She explained that she had lived and worked on a family farm then also at an egg plant in Wisconsin. That she just moved to California and was beginning her work search.

Sally exclaimed over the jazz band, "You're kidding me!" And in the excitement, she motioned over another couple to introduce them to Elizabeth Rose.

Sally jumped up to give Miriam a hug, and then pulled her over to the table, "Miriam, you won't believe it, this girl just moved here from Wisconsin and she has farm cooking experience. You know, cooking for lots of people who live on a farm."

Miriam sized up Elizabeth Rose before taking a seat next to her and extending her hand, "Miriam".

"Hi, I'm Elizabeth Rose."

Sally bent over to tell Elizabeth Rose, "Miriam works as the head housekeeper for a movie family here in Hollywood. She's looking for an assistant."

Over her shoulder she pointed to Miriam and her husband Floyd, "They both actually live there."

In excitement, Sally held Elizabeth Rose by the

shoulders, and began to jump up and down, "You'd be great at it." Then she grabbed her soldier date and ran off to the dance floor.

Floyd, who had been standing behind Miriam, stepped forward and stuck his hand out to introduce himself to Elizabeth Rose and the group. After a brief conversation, Miriam ended up inviting Elizabeth Rose to meet with her employers Monday morning, to interview for the assistant housekeeper position.

Tom and Elizabeth Rose hit the dance floor, proving to Tom she could cut a mean Foxtrot, Waltz and Two-step. With each twist and turn, they glided along the smooth, wooden floor with ease, falling more and more in love with each other.

The evening ended on a high note for both Elizabeth Rose and Rae. Tom asked Elizabeth Rose to wait for him while he was away. He promised to be faithful and true to her. Rae really hit it off with Frank who was a flight training instructor as well. It seemed that Elizabeth Rose made a new friend with Sally who invited her to keep in touch. She suggested that once she got settled, they would maybe do something together.

Elizabeth Rose had to take three different buses, but she arrived on time to her interview. Miriam was the head housekeeper to Hollywood producer and director, Mr. Lucca Pisoniano, and his wannabe actress wife, Anna. Anna was born Henrietta Thompson to a wealthy Nebraska banker. They were movers and shakers in the movie industry, known for their glitzy lifestyle and all night parties. Lucca was fifteen years Anna's senior.

Theirs was a marriage of convenience. If Lucca

couldn't find funding in Hollywood for a movie, he tapped Anna's father, and put her in the starring female role. Lucca had a slight upper-hand in the marriage with Anna's naivety about affairs of the heart and things that happened behind the scenes, even in her own home.

Anna spent a couple hours every week at her psychiatrist, but most of her days were spent getting facials, or her hair and nails done at the country club spa. Her pampering was under the guise of looking for talent and movie opportunities for her husband. It also kept them in touch with the scuttlebutt of the powerful Hollywood circles which she learned from other wives, girlfriends and mistresses of the movie moguls who would go to the same spas. While Anna was away, her husband Lucca took auditions at home or worked the golf greens and bars for movie making money and fresh raw talent he could exploit unless he was onset making a movie.

With Elizabeth Rose's farm cooking household experience, she was highly recommended by Miriam to the Pisoniano's, who hired her on the spot. She was to receive a weekly salary for her services and each week her hours could change depending on how they needed her.

Theirs was a life of high society, with the best in modern housing such as telephones in several rooms, indoor plumbing and electric lighting along with the latest gadgets and fashionable furnishings. Radio's and phonographs were scattered about the house as entertaining was essential to their lifestyle.

The backyard housed most of the events. With its Italian renaissance style, it was the epitome of excellence, complete with a bar and lounge area to accommodate guests, and a swimming pool surrounded by white marble Doric columns, imported from Italy. There was an area to accommodate a small band or quartet as well as an in house theater.

Even with the differences in affluence, Elizabeth Rose was ever so thankful to find work so fast. She was ambitious and didn't want to be over staying her welcome with Rae. Within a weeks' time she was able to secure a rental place of her own. It was a small, lower flat on the outskirts of town bordering on the area farm fields and orchards. And for the short time remaining that Tom would be stateside, it put her just a little bit closer to him.

The following week, Tom went to Europe. She saw him one last time before he departed. He gave her a relationship pin and a copy of his military picture. She reciprocated with a locket with her picture enclosed. These were keepsakes to remember each other by. They were both uneasy about his departure. The odds were stacked against him as a bomber pilot, but they tried to both be optimistic in the presence of each other for his eventual return.

Elizabeth Rose, in the beginning, thought she hit the jackpot working for the Hollywood up and comers. The first couple of days Miriam and her husband Floyd, who was the gardener and grounds keeper, were kind and cordial to her. They happily showed her around and started to pass off duties to her.

Miriam gloated about the stars she met while working for the Pisoniano's and explained how often Mr. Pisoniano would have them stop by for auditions.

Miriam shared with Elizabeth Rose some items she claimed Anna wanted discarded. These were teaser gifts to Elizabeth Rose. For most of the time, Miriam kept all the stuff herself.

Typical items discarded were articles of clothing like blouses, shoes, costume jewelry and occasionally some housewares or other insignificant gifts they received from others. One of the first things Miriam passed on to Elizabeth Rose was a bowl that had Egyptian images painted on it, that she claimed Anna wanted thrown out, because she didn't like the aspiring actress who gave it to her as a party gift.

Miriam's words to Elizabeth Rose on why she gave her the bowl were, "Yeah, Mrs. Pisoniano said to get rid of it. I don't need any more junk around my house, so I'm giving it to you."

Elizabeth Rose soon figured out that Miriam wasn't much of a trainer, and if anything, she turned out more to be a blamer. In the beginning, Elizabeth Rose wasn't given much training, just directives by Miriam. Then the complaints started to come in for Elizabeth Rose's work performance.

Miriam would tell Elizabeth Rose to "do this" and then after Elizabeth Rose did it wrong, Miriam then crossly scolded her "don't do that, do this" as when Anna fell apart after having her breakfast served wrong. Her eggs were not to touch her three pieces of bacon nor the toast and the plate was to be placed on the table with the eggs to the lower left and the bacon on the lower right.

Elizabeth Rose also found out the hard way that Anna preferred to have her bath towels tri-folded not half-folded. Elizabeth Rose just put these couple of bad experiences to learning the ropes and figured it would go much smoother with time.

With Tom being in service action in Europe, Sally

invited Elizabeth Rose to go to the movies one evening. She went to Sally's house to help her with her hair and was surprised to learn she had a young son. Little Joe was well-mannered and well behaved. His fine, dark hair was neatly combed in place with a clean side part.

While Elizabeth Rose helped Sally get ready, they had a bit of girl talk. Sally asked how Tom was doing. Elizabeth Rose shared that he made it through his first missions bombing the German Leftwaffe in France and that now he was under General Eisenhower's command, focused on disrupting the German supply chain of oil refineries, locomotives, and railcars, trucks and tanks.

Sally stated "You don't know how lucky you are to have such a good guy."

She then went on to share how at one time she was an aspiring actress. But when her son came along, she took the waitress job to have steady work.

Elizabeth Rose just took her comments in. Being the polite mid-westerner, she didn't want to pry about little Joe's father.

Then Sally tried to pump Elizabeth Rose on some of the goings on at the Pisoniano household. But Elizabeth Rose wouldn't give any details. It didn't feel right for her to gossip about her employer with Sally, especially when Miriam and Sally seemed to be such good friends.

The landlady came down to watch little Joe. With one last look in the mirror, Sally adjusted her hat. As she started to put her gloves on she looked over at Elizabeth Rose.

"Where are your gloves?"

Elizabeth Rose explained that she didn't bring any.

"A lady always should be seen out with her gloves."

To Elizabeth Rose, gloves were only to be worn during special occasions.

Sally went to her closet and pulled down a pair of gloves. "You can keep these as a thank you for helping me with my hair."

Sally got down on her knee to say goodbye to her "little pie in the sky" and kissed him on the cheek. The two women took off for the movie theater where Elizabeth Rose saw newsreel footage of the Allied front. The sight of all the casualties sent a chill down her spine.

At work the next day, Miriam was curious about Elizabeth Rose's night out with Sally. She was already sitting at the kitchen table, drinking her coffee and smoking her cigarettes. Some laundry was actually folded. And just as soon as she started to quiz Elizabeth Rose, the phone rang. It was Sally on the line.

Elizabeth Rose didn't want to be any part of whatever was going on. She could tell Miriam and Sally were talking about her, and in an effort to separate from their conversation, she grabbed her cleaning supplies and left the kitchen.

Flustered and feeling uneasy with all that had happened, she took a moment in the hallway to sort her supplies out and calm down. Her mind was racing and in an attempt to escape the negative vibes she was feeling, she hastily set about to begin cleaning.

Not thinking, she hurriedly headed to Mr. Pisoniano's office and forgot to knock on the door. Barging in, she found him in an early morning audition with a young starlet who was in a compromised position. Embarrassed, Elizabeth Rose immediately stopped in her tracks and apologized profusely. She hastily stepped backwards out of the room and swiftly shut the door behind her.

In the hallway, Elizabeth Rose turned to see Miriam standing in the kitchen doorway, coldly staring at her. It really wasn't turning out to be such a good morning for Elizabeth Rose, who red faced, grabbed her cleaning supplies and headed the other way down the hall. She was filled with fear, and the tight knot she felt in her stomach told her that her position at the Pisoniano's was possibly in jeopardy.

For the next couple months, Elizabeth Rose kept her nose to the grind stone and never spoke of the incident to Miriam at all. She also kept her distance from Sally. With time, Elizabeth Rose ended up being the main cleaner and cook in the house working up to twelve hours a day, seven days a week. With Tom being in action overseas, being busy was what Elizabeth Rose needed most at this time.

The only time Miriam seemed to expend herself was when a big dinner party was planned. These would end up being seventeen hour days for Elizabeth Rose, because she ended up doing all the cooking and assisted Miriam with the serving. Floyd doubled as the bartender at these events.

A couple days before the big Christmas party, Miriam and Floyd were having a marital argument in the kitchen. Floyd slapped Elizabeth Rose on the buttocks in front of Miriam and then tried to kiss her too. Elizabeth Rose was shocked and immediately left the room red faced. She didn't know what she did to be treated that way or put in the middle of their argument. Once Floyd left, she went back to the kitchen and tried to apologize to Miriam who, with a wave of her hand, walked away and out of the room.

In the beginning, Elizabeth Rose was in awe of seeing the B-List stars that would attend these parties, dressed in their minks and fine linen suits. Often they were bearing gifts of fine wines and cognacs or other trinkets of significant value.

But her awe quickly turned into disappointment when she saw the dirty games they played, and how under the influence their actions digressed as the evenings wore on. She quite often overheard the backstabbing conversations they would have about others in the room, typically within ear shot of the person they were insulting.

At one party, a young aspiring actor gave Anna and Lucca a brass whale paperweight vying for a role in Lucca's next seafaring movie. Anna openly criticized him for being so bold within his earshot. The comment ruined the young actor's evening, for the other attendees scattered, not wanting to be associated with him. It was as if he was chewed up and spit out of the belly of the whale.

The twelve hour days were tiring, but it helped to fill her day so she wasn't idly worrying about Tom, and it paid her rent. Elizabeth Rose tried to shut out all the negativity and just focus on her work. She was battling her feelings of being drained, worrying about Tom at the warfront in Europe and didn't want to be involved in all the Pisoniano household drama.

But Elizabeth Rose was starting to see through Miriam and how she and her husband Floyd were manipulating the Pisoniano's to their benefit. On the surface, Elizabeth Rose was always the fall guy for any mistakes or when something wasn't completed to the Pisoniano's satisfaction. It was Miriam, as head housekeeper, who took their directives and passed them off to Elizabeth Rose. But she often never fully shared the details. She was too busy sitting around filing her nails with the entertainment section of the newspaper spread out in front of her as she waited for the phone to ring. It was usually one of Mr. Pisoniano's starlet's calling to schedule auditions.

Unbeknownst to Anna, Miriam was coordinating Lucca's 'auditions' but these were typically conjugal visits of which Sally was sometimes one of them. That was one of the benefits for Mr. Pisoniano working out of his home while his wannabe actress wife was out to the spa, or at her acting lessons, or meeting with her singing or dance coach.

Elizabeth Rose surmised that on some level Mr. Pisoniano paid dearly for Miriam and Floyd's silence regarding his audition practices but she wasn't quite sure how.

One week after the Christmas party, Elizabeth Rose arrived to work surprised to find Miriam with little Joe in the kitchen. She stupidly asked if Sally was there, to which Miriam rolled her eyes at her, then redirected her attention to little Joe.

Elizabeth Rose didn't say anything, but just left the kitchen and got to work. However, her thoughts were churning. With her dust rag in hand, she overheard the loud moans coming from Mr. Pisoniano's study. Anger sprang up inside her as she thought about little Joe sitting in the kitchen, waiting patiently for his mother.

Later that morning, Elizabeth Rose ran into Sally and Mr. Pisoniano who were in the kitchen by little

Joe and Miriam. He was making small talk with little Joe then handed a bumpy envelope to Sally with something in it for her. Miriam's and Elizabeth Rose's eyes met. Elizabeth Rose knew all too well the hard life that little boy was going to face being classified as an illegitimate, bastard child.

Things were quiet for a couple weeks around the Pisoniano household, although it seemed things were amiss between Elizabeth Rose and Miriam ever since the arguing incident in which Floyd tried to kiss her. Elizabeth Rose also sensed that Anna suspected something was going on with her husband and other women, but Miriam was an expert at covering up for Mr. Pisoniano's activities.

On her bus ride home, Elizabeth Rose was tired and stressed out from all the craziness at work and also because she was worried about Tom. She saw potential relief coming at work with the Pisoniano's going to Nebraska to see Anna's family over the holidays.

Someone conveniently left a newspaper on the seat next to her. Today's headlines were unsettling with the latest news on the Battle of the Bulge underway and the campaign in the Pacific against Japan. She had been avoiding reading the papers lately because she didn't want to get caught up in the sad news of all the casualties and fuel her worry about Tom's safety over in Europe.

Instead, she studied a photo of a Japanese suicide plane crash in the Pacific in which several American service men died on a ship at sea. She sympathized with how those men must have felt helpless as they saw the plane descending upon them.

The news of the day seemed to support her

internal stirring that she needed to do something about her life and work situation, that she was a sitting target of some sort. She felt it was a warning that if she continued to drift along by staying employed at the Pisoniano household, that her source of income was going to be taken from her somehow, and she needed to do something to protect herself. She took the newspaper with her to start looking for new employment and hoped the search would alleviate some of the tension she felt in her life. She just didn't feel right and deep inside, she knew something was askew.

Later that evening, while she bathed, Elizabeth Rose scanned the paper and circled some possible places to apply for work. Sunday was typically a short day for her and she was hoping to stop by and see Rae. She hadn't seen her in a while and was going to ring her first thing in the morning to arrange a visit to meet her. With tomorrow being Saturday, she wanted to make sure Rae was available first before she made the bus trip over.

After settling into bed, she gave thanks for the things she was appreciative for that day even though at work it was hard to be positive. She then prayed for Tom's safety.

But something just didn't feel right. She recalled what her Grandma Friedrich and Jade had repeatedly told her to do, to listen to her heart. Elizabeth Rose tried to separate the emotion from all that was going on in her life but nothing was clear. She knew she had to see Rae, her true friend, and talk some things through with her. Because deep inside her, Elizabeth Rose's heart was trying to tell her something was wrong, and not to stay where she was with the

Pisoniano's. Her last words before she drifted off to sleep were "Please God, bring me a new job."

Morning came and Elizabeth Rose was not rested at all. All night she tossed and turned, worried about things in her life she couldn't seem to control. Rae said it was coincidental to hear from her because she was going to call Elizabeth Rose as well. Rae wanted to see her and Frank did too.

Elizabeth Rose was relieved that she would be able to see her old friend so soon. She didn't want to step into that Pisoniano household one more time. The lack of morality on a daily basis was more than she could handle. But yet she needed to work to cover her bills. Plus she had Christmas presents to pay for and post to her family back home, along with packages to Jade and Tom.

Disheartened energy over took Elizabeth Rose as she entered through the servants entry way. She noticed that breakfast had already appeared to be made, so she set about gathering her supplies for her daily duties. In her mind, she just assumed they were getting an early start to their day, due to their travels to Nebraska.

Once she opened up the kitchen door, she found Miriam and Floyd waiting for her in the hallway, just off of the dining area. She approached them to find Anna and Lucca already at the table having breakfast.

"Elizabeth" Mr. Pisoniano called her over to the table with a wave of a couple of his fingers.

Hesitantly, Elizabeth Rose replied "Yes" while glancing over at Miriam and Floyd. Floyd looked away while Miriam gave her a glare.

While looking down his nose, as he poured syrup

on his pancakes, he began in his Italian accent, "My wife has brought to my attention that her ruby and sapphire necklace has gone missing. Do you know anything about it?"

"Why no sir," she clearly stated, shaking her head and then glancing over at Miriam and Floyd, both of whom wouldn't look at her.

Anna injected, "But you're the only one who dusts my things and you were the last one Miriam saw touch my jewelry box."

Elizabeth Rose turned to sternly look at Miriam. Miriam just sneered back at her.

"But it wasn't me," Elizabeth Rose retorted.

"That will be all," he solemnly stated in his broken accent.

Distraught, Elizabeth Rose called out, "But I swear to you, it wasn't me"

"Please give her pay envelope to her and escort her out." Mr. Pisoniano gave a wave with the backside of his hand, as if to shoo her away.

Floyd stepped forward, handed her the envelope and grabbed her by the arm. Miriam followed as they walked out.

Angered by what happened, Elizabeth Rose and Miriam had a few last words at the backdoor.

"You set me up."

"You were starting to know too much. And with a mouth like that, I will make sure you never work in this town again, as a servant to the elite of Hollywood."

Defiant, Elizabeth Rose blasted back "After this experience, I don't want to ever again." She turned on her heels and walked away with her head held high.

Floyd added "Oh, lordy. She's a feisty one."

Shaken, Elizabeth Rose felt numb inside during the bus ride home. She couldn't believe what had just happened. It was all too surreal. Anger started to build inside her as she thought through how she was played by Miriam into always being the bad guy. And with a deep breathe she calmed herself down by realizing she was free now from the negativity of their social charades. She straightened up her stance, and told herself she wasn't going to let Miriam, Floyd or the Pisoniano's get her down. She set her mind to applying to some of the jobs she had circled in the Friday paper.

Quickly, she stopped off at home to freshen up her look and pick up the newspaper. She left her house with her head held high and a smile on her face. She was determined she wasn't going to let them beat her.

POWERISMS

✤ **Power of Repetitive Experiences:** Experiences are repeated until the lesson is learned. Often times, all you need to do is recognize the pattern and when in the circumstance again, decline to get involved or take action to separate from the situation.

✤ **Power of Thought as Initial Catalyst:** Any intuitive, spontaneous thought can protect you as in times of possible harm, or propel you forward and open new doors of opportunity for you. However, negative self-talk, whether thought or even if just spoken "off the cuff', can hold you back and hinder your progression. Listen to your own internal guidance and watch you words!

POWER TOOL

✎ **Change in Feelings:** When your feelings change, it can set in motion a new direction for your life. It is a sign that you have a new desire. Action is required to harmonize your values with your change in emotions and new goals.

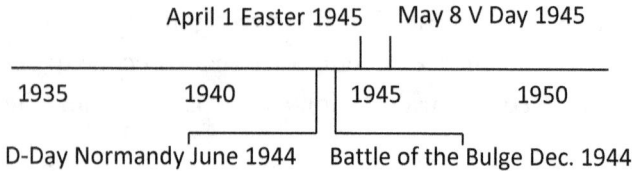

April 1 Easter 1945   May 8 V Day 1945

1935   1940   1945   1950

D-Day Normandy June 1944   Battle of the Bulge Dec. 1944

6 LIFE OF PURPLE

The grocery store was all a hustle and bustle with people grocery shopping for Christmas. Luckily, Elizabeth Rose was able to immediately meet with the manager of the Kroger store who hired her on the spot. He was impressed with her look, and being from the Midwest, he surmised she had a good work ethic. He offered her an hourly wage as a checker and asked her to train right away if she could. He needed extra help for the holidays and he said he would even be able to give her overtime if she was willing to work it. By 9am Elizabeth Rose had lost a job and found another. By the end of her first shift she was efficiently checking out customers on her own.

At dinner on Sunday, Elizabeth Rose saw how close Frank and Rae were becoming. Frank shared details on the war effort and confirmed some of the events that Tom had written her about. With the Allied front in full gear, he was extremely busy training new troops to be sent off in support of the Allies.

Compared to previous jobs Elizabeth Rose held, she found it easy to be working at Kroger. She loved conversing with the regular customers. The store manager appreciated her and she was treated fairly by the other clerks. In fact, one of the other checkout girls, Viola, invited Elizabeth Rose to her house for a Christmas party.

Elizabeth Rose officially lost Sally as a friend, but questioned if she ever really was a friend. She never talked to her again after she was fired from the Pisoniano's. She surmised that the lumpy envelope he gave her that day in the kitchen contained the necklace, which he used for child alimony hush money.

The weekly letters from Tom helped Elizabeth Rose remain hopeful for his safe return. With her new work schedule, she was able to see Rae and Frank more often. These visits helped alleviate her loneliness and made her feel connected to Tom, even though he was so far away.

Rae and Frank invited Elizabeth Rose to go with them to the Palladium for New Year's Eve. They were doing a live broadcast for the troops overseas. Elizabeth Rose danced a few dances with some of the Army guys Frank knew, but otherwise she pretty much kept to the table, from where she looked out on the dancers and observed the band. It was turning into a reflective and somber evening for her as she recalled the events of the last year. How she stood up for herself against her abusive Uncle Samuel and bravely took the train out to California. She thought about the nice sailor McEvoy, she had met on the Milwaukee train to Chicago, and prayed he was still alive at sea.

She wondered how Catherine was doing and whether she got her Christmas card. Elizabeth Rose said another prayer that her fiancé was still alive and then softly smiled when she recalled how it was Catherine that first noticed Tom looking at her. All Elizabeth Rose wanted was an engagement ring from Tom, like Catherine had from her fiancé.

Under the table, Elizabeth Rose reached in her purse and pulled out the military picture of Tom he had given her before he departed. She quickly put it back in so no one would notice her being sentimental. She wondered where he had celebrated the eve of the New Year, so far away. She wondered who he was with and if he had thought of her.

Elizabeth Rose changed her attention to searching for Rae and Frank on the dance floor. She spotted them doing the waltz, his arm around her waist and them gazing eye-to-eye. Elizabeth Rose felt Rae was the lucky one for she was dating a soldier who was stateside. With the daily tally of casualties, she was starting to feel the numbers were against her, for Tom truly returning home to her. Tom's letters were starting to reflect his weariness of the war as well. But she didn't want to give up hope. There was always a chance he would make it home to her.

Elizabeth Rose recalled how a couple nights ago she was lying in bed thinking of Tom when she felt a click in her stomach- sort of like a string snapped. She didn't like what she felt but ever since then she once again sensed something was wrong. A foreboding feeling loomed about, and her muscles were tight in her stomach. All night she struggled with hiding her feelings from Rae, Frank and the others. She just prayed deep in her heart that he was alright.

With the New Year celebration over, there was a decrease in grocery shoppers. All day at work, she was befuddled by a nagging feeling of uneasiness in her stomach that just never seemed to leave her. To add to these feelings, there was news of massive plane losses during the 1945 New Year's Day German attacks on Allied Airfields and this news fueled her anxiety. She just couldn't shake the ill feeling.

Unbeknownst to her, Rae had called her manager to ask what time Elizabeth Rose was done with work. Rae and Frank walked in as she was handing her cash drawer over to her manager. The instant she saw them, a wave of sadness overtook her but she retained her composure. Her manager offered her to take the day off tomorrow if she needed it, but Elizabeth Rose stubbornly declined.

Rae stretched out her hand to give Elizabeth Rose a handkerchief as she approached. She took it from her and bowed her head as she kept walking out the door. She didn't want the others to see her cry.

In Frank's car, Rae tried to comfort her. After a few minutes, Elizabeth Rose's crying subsided. She realized how she had seen other women crying in vehicles, crying over dead soldiers and she didn't want to make a spectacle of herself, standing out as one of them too.

For dinner, Frank picked up some fried chicken and beer in honor of Tom – it was his favorite meal. With a full belly, and time spent with Rae and Frank, her emotions calmed down although the news still stinged. She phoned her manager that evening and confirmed with him she would be in to work tomorrow. She stated that she really wanted to be around people and not at home feeling sorry for herself. Rae and Frank actually spent the night, opting to get up bright and early to make their jobs the next morning. Elizabeth Rose was grateful for their company, but was ready to be on her own to process the loss of Tom.

At work the next day, Elizabeth's co-workers were all very concerned and consoling. Viola offered up, "Honey, whatever you need, I am here for you. Just ask." The news quickly spread to customers who expressed their condolences as well.

With the holidays over, Elizabeth Rose found she actually had more free-time but unfortunately, she also found that during any time of unplanned idleness, she found herself frequently fretting over the loss of Tom. She forced herself to finally meet her neighbors.

On one side of her lived a man who seemed to be of an odd sort. He seemed even odder when she learned his name. Mr. Coffin was an actuarial, who promptly left every day at 8:30am and returned home most days by 5:30pm. He was of a fair statue being not too tall nor too short. His hair was always neatly cut and combed, and his suits impeccably pressed with shoes polished to a high gloss shine. His simple yard was expertly groomed as well, but void of color or flowering plants. He was a no-nonsense sort of person who cordially greeted Elizabeth Rose each time he saw her. He mostly kept to himself but seemed to keep a watchful eye on her by the things he inquired about during their small talk.

On the other side lived a man who seemed to be even odder than Mr. Coffin. She was told by Mr. Coffin that this neighbor was a professional wrestler that went by the name of Gorgeous George. He traveled a lot so was often times not at home. By the looks of his property, he had a thing for the color purple although Elizabeth Rose didn't ask Mr. Coffin about his colorful yard.

The chill of February just wouldn't leave the air. The days and nights seemed to drag on as Elizabeth Rose tried to keep her life together. With not getting the over time like she did during the holidays, she tried to be frugal with her money and this added to the long, lonely nights. She struggled with moving forward from Tom and putting herself out there. Viola and some of the other Kroger co-workers invited her to the Paladium where Lawrence Welk was playing. He and his band were filming at one of the movie studios.

The hall was full of military men, looking to have some fun before they were to be sent overseas. Most were being deployed to the pacific with the war against Japan heating up.

A young Marine was full of alcohol and full of himself as he danced his way over to their table. He said blankly, "Hi ladies, I'm Rick O'Shea. Anyone care for a dance?" He already had his sights set on Elizabeth Rose and without hesitation, took her by the hand and dragged her out to the dance floor. Elizabeth Rose didn't even have a chance to respond to him.

He swung her around and they came face-to-face for the waltz. With each step he breathed harder and harder. The smell of alcohol permeated his presence and Elizabeth Rose had to turn her head so she would avoid the full assault of his halitosis.

To make small-talk he asked, "You come here often?"

She took a breath before turning her head to answer, "No, I've never been here before."

"Me too." A little bit of spit sprayed out and Elizabeth Rose just cringed as it hit the side of her face. She wanted to be nice but his drunkenness was almost unbearable.

She thanked him for the dance when the song was over, thinking he would be on his way, but he followed her back to the table. He sat down and tried to join in the conversation. He felt compelled to tell the women that he has never mortally committed a sin. It was clear he was having doubts and fear about following orders and fulfilling his solider duties.

At the end of the night, he insisted on giving Elizabeth Rose his General Douglas MacArthur lapel button. He wanted her to have a memento for her to remember him by. After he pinned it on her dress, he got all handsy with her and tried to kiss her.

Elizabeth Rose pushed him back exclaiming, "Get off of me!" She followed with a hard smack of her hand on the side of his face. He was surprised at how strong she was and the sting of her slap quickly sobered him up a bit.

She finished by stating, "I don't move that fast. I am definitely not that type of a girl."

Viola and the others had seen what happened and came to her rescue. They all walked out together leaving Rick O'Shea to nurse his wounds alone in the dance hall.

Each passing day, the weather seemed to be getting a little warmer and the season seemed to be changing. Elizabeth Rose went to work every day, numbly moving forward. She was still hurt and processing all that had happened with Tom. She understood he was dead and there was nothing she could do, but she just couldn't understand why it happened to her. She had a fortress built up around her and she was trying her best to make herself available although she declined going on arranged dates by Frank. She didn't want to date another pilot and endure the worry and wonder if he would ever return. And she just didn't feel comfortable dating someone that possibly knew Tom or to be unfairly judged by some of his other Army buddies for trying to move on to soon.

With the Easter holiday approaching, the store manager was busy building displays of Easter Lilly plants and canned Spam. The doors were propped open allowing the gentle breezes to funnel through, freshening up the remains of the dull, stale winter air. It was a nice break from the cool dreariness that had been blanketing the skies.

The change in weather, combined with the progress the Allied front was making in the Pacific and Europe, seemed to lift everyone's spirit. Even Elizabeth Rose seemed to lose the glum that had been hanging over her. All her sad thoughts of her life the last few months had dissipated with the clouds. Everyone's jovial disposition seemed to radiate as the day wore on.

After lunch, Elizabeth Rose was talking with one of the regular shoppers she was checking out when she caught a glimpse of a handsome naval officer entering the grocery store. They made eye contact for a brief minute to which Elizabeth Rose grinned at him. He turned back to give her a second look and walked right into the fancy display of Spam that the store manager spent a couple hours building that morning.

Elizabeth Rose anticipated his demise and immediately threw her hands up over her eyes as if not seeing would help save the handsome, dashing naval officer from harm. The noise of cans tumbling down rumbled throughout the store and startled the customers.

Elizabeth Rose peaked through her fingers to see him standing there quite embarrassed and distraught at the mayhem he caused.

She started to laugh and called out to him, "Careful! Don't want you to get hurt!"

The store manager ran up to see where all the commotion was coming from and found the naval officer hastily trying to restack the cans.

"No worries Petty Officer."

"Pierson, Petty Officer Pierson."

"I'll get this," the store manager told him.

After the can debacle was under control, Petty Officer Pierson took his leave of the store, but made sure to turn back to catch Elizabeth Rose's attention and gave her a nod and a wave good-bye.

The encounter with the naval officer reignited the romance spark in Elizabeth Rose. Each day she awoke hoping she would see him again. But days turned into weeks and he never made his way back in to the grocery store. Her imposter self and rambling mind started to fill her with thoughts that she wasn't good enough for a loving relationship.

On her next day off, Elizabeth Rose was feeling exceptionally down. In an attempt to overcome these feelings, she threw herself into cooking and cleaning her house, plus doing laundry. First, she mixed up some bread dough to let rise and then began washing some clothes. With the laundry on the line, she put the bread in the oven to bake then made some cookies. As the cookies baked she began sweeping up the crumbs in the kitchen and eventually the whole house. She shook the crumbs and other debris off the rugs outside then checked the laundry drying on the clothes lines. She felt like a yo-yo with being in and out of the house so many times throughout the day.

That evening, she was nearly done cleaning up in the kitchen with washing, drying and putting away the dishes, when she came across the Egyptian bowl that Miriam had passed off to her. She had stuck it up in the top cupboard to get it out of the way. It bothered her every time she looked at it. She recalled the day she found her friend, Jade, doing some spring cleaning and how she had gotten rid of things that had an emotional sting attached to them.

She got the step stool out to pull the bowl down. Setting it on the counter, she gave it a spin to turn it and look at the detail painted on the outside. Every time she looked at the bowl it reminded her of when Miriam's husband, Floyd, had tried to kiss her in front of Miriam. Then she recalled how Miriam, her husband Floyd, and Mr. Pisoniano had set her up by taking the fall for Mrs. Pisoniano's missing sapphire and ruby necklace. The emotional sting of those embarrassments still hurt her. Even though it was a perfectly fine pottery bowl, she knew it was time to get rid of it. She no longer wanted to hang on to those feelings.

Then she remembered the gloves that Sally had given her. On a roll of cleaning up her house and clearing out the negativity, she immediately headed to the closet. Of course, she had thrown them on the back of the shelf. Exhausted, she didn't want to make a trip back to the kitchen to get the step stool so Elizabeth Rose proceeded to jump up to try and grab them. The second attempt she pulled a little too hard on the shelf and down it came along with all its contents. The wooden shelf hit her squarely in the forehead between her eyebrow and hairline.

The force of the blow set her back a moment and she immediately applied pressure to her forehead, all the while wincing from the pain of the impact. This wasn't the way she wanted to end her day. With her hand, she applied pressure to the wound when she felt some blood trickled through her fingers. She made her way to the bathroom to give the injury a better look. Thankfully there was only a little gash above her eyebrow that she put a clean cloth on for a few minutes to stop the blood flow.

After affixing a bandage, she immediately set back to her task at hand. She was on a mission to remove all the hurt in her life, not wanting a little bump on her head to slow her down. She was done with those old feelings of hurt from Sally and Miriam. She felt by getting rid of the visual reminders, she was one step closer to forgetting them so they wouldn't emotionally interfere in her life again. As she bent over to pull the gloves out of the chaos, she felt a little off balance and had to grab the closet door handle. She needed to steady herself and noticed as she stood back up, that her head started to throb.

Feeling a little light headed and a little nauseous, Elizabeth Rose went to take a break in the living room. She set the gloves on the end table then laid down on the sofa. The remaining sunlight of the day streamed in the windows, so she shielded her eyes. All she wanted was to get rid of the things that distressed her and caused her pain whenever she looked at them. And it's ironic how she caused herself pain in trying to get rid of those things. Right now, more than anything, she wanted those things and the people associated with them out of her life. With having to rest from the dizziness of her forehead injury, it seemed like she was being held back and it was making her angry.

Exhaustion and stress consumed her as she lay on the sofa. With sunset a short time away, her bed was calling and the closet shelf contents could wait to be picked up another day. An icepack was in order to help ease the pain of her head injury.

She mustered up the strength to sit up. Gently, she caressed the bandage on her forehead and then shook her head as if to kick herself for letting the stupid gloves from Sally push her so hard that she hurt herself. She scooped up the gloves and gingerly walked to the kitchen, tossing them in the Egyptian bowl on the counter. She began her quest to find the ice pack and in the process of finding it stuffed in the back of a drawer, saw the Douglas MacArthur button that Rick O'Shea had given her at the dance that night he pushed himself on her. She threw that in the bowl as well.

After filling the ice pack, she started to shut her house for the night, pulling down all the blinds and locking the doors. She quivered a little when she noticed Mr. Coffin sitting in his living room reading the evening paper. For some reason, he reminded her of something she was trying to avoid, something that tied in to a memory of Jade's spring cleaning. That she needed to let go of the letters from Tom, too. But she just didn't feel emotionally strong enough to do it tonight.

Feeling defeated, she made a stop in the bathroom where she noticed she had underestimated the extent of her injury by the size of the welt on her head. She prayed to God she wouldn't have a black eye but she could see a red-purple hue starting to form on her forehead.

With her night gown on, she headed to her bedroom. Before pulling down her bedroom blind, she took a minute to look out her window at wrestler, Gorgeous George's house. He must have returned home for his lights were on. She wondered about him and why he had everything in purple on his property. She decided that tomorrow was going to be the day that she went over and found out why, but for now she had to get off to bed.

After settling into bed, Elizabeth Rose began her daily review by finding things she was appreciative for that day.

"Angels," she said, "I had a great day cleaning and clearing. Thank you for helping me to clear all this negativity out of my life. Help me to release any emotional attachments that remain that no longer serve me." She didn't even want to say Tom's name out loud. "I only want to gaze upon items of neutrality or that remind me of love."

All in all, she felt indifferent before drifting off to sleep. It was as if she was afraid to feel because of all the past emotional hurts she was still carrying inside. She didn't want to think about these feelings because she didn't know what thoughts would help get her out of this conundrum. All she knew was that she wanted to know the story behind George's purple obsession.

Gorgeous George the wrestler lived a life of purple. Everything on his property was purple. As she gazed at his place on her walk over she saw his purple Buick sedan in his yard and knew he was still home. She slid her wicker basket to her elbow area so she could open his fence gate. He had painted the fencing around his yard different shades of purple. His house was painted purple and she studied the purple pansies mixed in with yellow ones for contrast that he had planted along the stone path leading up to his porch.

Smoothing her dress, she took in a deep breath, before knocking on his door. She noticed the wood trim was a deeper shade of purple that accented the overall lilac house color. She heard footsteps approaching.

George answered his door with a look of surprise on his face. Of course, he was wearing a purple shirt and pants. He looked Elizabeth Rose over, who immediately introduced herself and offered him the basket of bread and sugar cookies she just baked the day before. He thanked her and invited her in for some tea.

Leading her to his living room, he invited her to take a seat and then he went off to the kitchen to fetch the tea. While waiting, she noticed that many of his furnishings were purple too, such as his drapes, sofa and chairs except for the wood accents and wood floors. He had pictures on the walls of him wrestling that were in purple, painted frames. She could tell by the various locations of the pictures that he had traveled a lot during his career.

When he came back she asked, "George, why is everything purple?"

"I live a life of purple," he explained. "I live to my highest potential, tapping into my highest self to achieve and be all that I can be, to the best of my ability."

He poured some tea into the teacups, which had purple flowers on them.

"I learned it all from visiting the keeper of the power house."

Gorgeous George pointed out the window toward the hydro-power plant that stood up at the plateau on the Mountain of Life and overlooked the valley. The white steam was pouring up out of the power plant stacks. She knew the power plant was a generator of energy but did not know its keeper held such wisdoms. She also recalled occasionally seeing different colored puffs of steam released from the stack.

"It was a hard trip up the mountain, but well worth the journey. I strongly encourage you to go meet with the keeper. He is a great wealth of knowledge that can help any lost soul."

Elizabeth Rose was perplexed as to why he referred to her as a lost soul and wondered how he could know from just meeting her that she was struggling inside. She enjoyed learning more about George and his wrestling career and all the places he had traveled to for wrestling. She even learned a little bit more about what the power plant keeper did for

George and now she was curious to see if the keeper could help her too.

POWERISMS

❋ **Power of Desire:** Desire is based in an emotion and is an urge that leads to change. Something is lacking in your life and signals there will be realignment of an emotion, value or goal.

❋ **Power of Challenges:** When determination is used to overcome challenges, life changes occur. Could be a way to alert you to choose another path.

❋ **Power of Exercise:** Exercise puts your mind on a different focus, allowing things to be processed in the background and solutions to develop. Also, exercise releases endorphins that improve a person's mood state.

POWER TOOL

🔨 **Power of Imposter Self:** It's the negative internal voice that tells you you're not good enough, or that you can't succeed. It comes from a fear of failure or rejection and may be based on a past event. An individual may not realize they have these sabotaging, self-defeating thoughts. Once recognized, a change in mindset can be implemented including use of words and thoughts that support this change, along with action and risk taking to not only achieve a desired outcome but deactivate this negative internal voice.

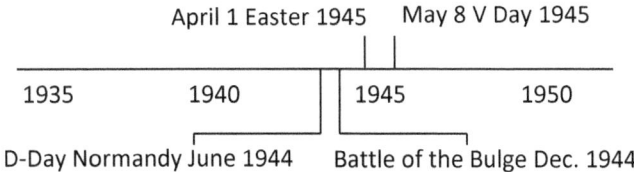

April 1 Easter 1945   May 8 V Day 1945

| 1935 | 1940 | 1945 | 1950 |

D-Day Normandy June 1944   Battle of the Bulge Dec. 1944

7 MEETING THE POWER PLANT KEEPER

After breakfast with George, Elizabeth Rose took his advice and set out to journey up to the Power Plant of Knowledge. To climb the winding, steep, upward path took much energy and determination. For the trip she put on pants and flat leather shoes and donned a cantina over her shoulder.

The first part of her journey was easy. It was flat, green grassy areas that led to the foot of Life Mountain. The late morning April sun was warming up the day with no wind. Chickadees and finches greeted her on the way. Once she hit the mountain trail, it started at first to wind back and forth with a slight incline. Butterflies such as copper gossamers, monarchs, yellow sulphur and swallowtails fluttered about as if to wish her well on her journey.

A couple hours into the hike, the trail was getting steeper. She found a scraggly old pine tree to take a break under and have a drink of water from her cantina. While under the shade of the tree, she took a moment to look around but didn't see much because she seemed to be in the thick of the trees. Cardinals were chirping around her and she saw a pair fluttering about from limb to limb.

As she continued on the steep, upward climb, danger seemed to lurk behind every corner that the trail turned. It wasn't very far up the trail that she encountered a bobcat. He was equally startled and stopped immediately in his tracks. His eyes widened at the sight of her and he immediately took off running for the trees. The encounter was brief, but scary enough to make her think about looking for a big stick to carry with her for protection. She remembered how on the foster farm she had a similar encounter and she wanted to have something to fight back with if needed. A short distance up the trail, she found a broken branch which she easily broke a couple smaller branches off of and the knobs served as a nice resting place for her hand.

At the midway point up the mountain, she found a big boulder with a flat surface that the sun had heated up. She climbed upon it to soak the heat into her leg muscles and rest for a while. Resting back on one elbow, she spied a long eared owl, who was silently observing her every move. She beamed at the sight of him and felt it was as if he was watching over her. She hadn't seen an owl since she left the farm.

Her gaze turned to the mountain side below, and she gaped at the sight of all the fallen down trees, rough terrain, and thick old foliage she had come through not to mention the rocky areas full of big boulders. She sat in disbelief at all she had come through and wondered if she made a rational decision in trying to make this journey on her own.

The owl started to restlessly flap its wings. It seemed to be signaling danger to her and she grabbed her stick to ready herself. Then she heard the faint noises of two bears battling each other down below. Elizabeth Rose stood up on the flat boulder and caught a glimpse of them batting each other about 200 feet away. The owl took off in flight and some other birds squawked their disproval at the commotion.

Not wasting any time, she jumped off the rock and made haste up the trail to distance herself from them. Then the trail suddenly encountered a swift running stream that had gained momentum from the steep mountain top above. She abruptly stopped and considered all options before venturing forward. She was left with no choice but to keep following the path she had started on. It looked as if she could follow the stream either going up or down on the same side but it wasn't as clear a trail as what she saw on the other side. In the distance, she heard the rumblings of the bears still duking it out below. She figured it was about 25 feet across to the other side with occasional rocks that stuck out which she could maybe use to hop on and pass over the shallow, swift moving water of the stream.

Tossing her concerns aside, she made the plunge and began to cross the stream. Her shoes were soaked with the first couple steps before she could start hopping onto the rocks. Her pant legs started to soak up some of the water and her leather soles were slightly slippery on the smooth polished stones. A couple times her footing slipped and she found herself in ankle deep, cool water that was sort of exhilarating and sent a flash of clarity throughout her body, especially clearing her mind. Once she got to the other side she took a moment to catch her breath and to take a look at the stream she just crossed. At this point, there was no turning back for Elizabeth Rose.

Exhaustion was overtaking her as she continued her trek. The climb was getting steeper and steeper, but yet her destination was insight. She couldn't stop now nor did she want to for all the danger that lurked about in the thick of the mountain vegetation. Up above, she could see the flat plateau of Life Mountain where the power plant stood.

It was hard to take her eyes off the trail for the fragile soil was prone to break away under the pressure of her steps. Occasionally, when she stole a quick glimpse to look back down the mountain, she was surprised at how steep the climb was and how many boulders she had to climb over to make her way toward the plant. She just couldn't understand why from the valley below, it seemed like such a lush, green covered hill with gently sloping sides and a cute little power plant on top. But in fact, it was full of danger from animals and rough terrain with vertical climbs and loose rocks along the way.

But she kept pushing on, not wanting to waste a precious moment of afternoon light. The sooner she got there, the safer she would feel. Then she questioned if the keeper would have any help or aid to offer her and she doubted her sanity in taking this trip alone.

A female eagle in a nest started to protest as she climbed closer but she just ignored it, staying fully focused on her footing and the trail. Then out of the corner of her eye, she caught the male eagle swooping down and at first she thought it was after her. Then she saw a raccoon shimming down the side of the tree, defeated in his attempt at a tasty meal of eggs. She half laughed to herself, remembering how on the farm they were such a nuisance, always trying to break into the chicken coop to steal eggs.

Thick foliage and wild growing young trees were the last obstacles to reaching the plateau. She had to grab onto the vines and young trunks to pull her body through them. Once she finally made the crest of the mountain, she lay on the grassy plateau for a few minutes to recuperate her strength. She noticed her legs and arms were shaking from the intense climb and her breathing was labored. With shaky hands, she fumbled to open her cantina for the last bit of water that remained. She put a little in her hand to wash over her face then took her shirt sleeve to wipe her face dry. Her muscles in her lower back and legs ached as she stood up. It was the most intense workout she had in a while and was comparable to hay harvest time with loading the bales of hay from the fields into the barn loft.

But it was all worth it once her eyes scanned the horizon and she saw the vast majesty of the valley. She could see clearly across to the other mountain range and the entire town in the valley below. Her home was easy to spot next door to Gorgeous George's purple palace.

She was amazed at her progress, at how far she had climbed up that day, and in how treacherous the path she had taken had been that had finally gotten her there.

Birds were chirping all around her and butterflies gently glided by as if to greet Elizabeth Rose at the crest of the mountain. She saw the power plant for the first time on the same level. It was much smaller than she thought it would be for it seemed so tall when she looked up at it from below. The concrete walls were painted a pristine, bright white and the stacks were gently releasing moist steam that dissipated in the sky. She heard the rumbling of the rushing waters that cascaded down from the upper peak of the Mountain of Life and pooled into the backside of the hydro power plant.

The grounds area was expertly landscaped all around the power house. Someone obviously spent a great deal of time taking care of this area. Everything was primped and trimmed; the trees, the hedges and the flower beds. The groomed grounds were accented with angelic and Romanesque statues, and benches throughout. There was even a koi fish reflecting pond.

She saw a bright red door that appeared to be the main entrance to the power house. Hummingbirds and butterflies escorted her as she followed the small walkway that led up to the big door. Once Elizabeth Rose stood on the stoop, the big red wooden door seemed overpowering. The door knocker and peep window was up above her head. With extreme trepidation she reached up and grabbed the heavy door knocker. She knocked on the door three times. Dong, Dong, Dong, the knocker echoed back at her.

She waited. Anxiety began to fill her. She questioned her good judgment in venturing all the way up to the top of this mountain to visit a man she had never met before. Her hands began to sweat and her breathing became rapid and shallow. She was hyperventilating. It seemed like she couldn't catch her breathe when suddenly; she heard footsteps from the other side of the door. The closer the person got the more fear filled her inside. She heard a man grumbling from the other side.

"Who in their right mind would be bothering me way up here?" she heard him question out loud.

The sounds of door locks could be heard and then the peep window of the door opened first.

"Who's there?" he grumbled out loud.

All she could see were two huge magnified blue eyes. He was wearing thick, round rimless glasses that made his eyes appear larger than they were. His messy, salt and pepper hair gave the impression he got ready in a hurry and he had a frown on his face, as if she had disturbed him.

"Hi, I'm Elizabeth Rose" she introduced herself. "Gorgeous George sent me to see you."

"Gorgeous George?" he gruffly questioned her back.

"He lives a life of purple" she reminded him.

"George?" he questioned back, "purple?" After a moment of pondering he recalled him.

"Oh, yes. George. Come in. Come in" he instructed her as he opened up the door. "How is he doing?" he inquired as the door loudly squeaked on the iron latches when he swung it open.

As she entered, she took in the full sight of the keeper. His hands were strong and he had long, lanky legs with broad shoulders and strong biceps. His gruff demeanor turned to gentle, caring, kindness.

"He's doing exceptionally well and thought I could benefit from some of your wisdom."

The keeper was locking the door back up, "Oh, he's a very kind man for saying that but I am just an overseer of the power house." He picked up the flashlight to light the way and gave a wave of his hand toward the inside of the plant, "Follow me."

Elizabeth Rose thought it odd that he would have a flash light and not turn the lights on. After all it was the inside of a power plant, but she didn't question him on it.

After climbing a long flight of stairs, he led Elizabeth Rose into a small room. The room faced south and had a big window with a rounded arch top that looked back down over the valley below. Above the window was written:

'Beauty is truth, truth is beauty, – that is all
Ye know on earth, and all ye need to know.'
John Keats 1795-1821.

She just assumed it was in reference to the beautiful view of the valley below. Her eyes continued to span around the room and she noticed all sorts of other sayings and words written on the walls such as words of wisdom, spiritual truths and lists of emotions and values.

Under the window, there was a table with two chairs on which pen and paper laid. He pulled a chair out for her stating, "Come, sit," as he motioned to her. "This is my guest room."

She took her cantina off from over her shoulder and strapped it over the back of the chair. She noticed the small cot pushed up against the inside wall of the room next to a kitchen utility cart with a few food items and a pitcher of water and a couple drinking glasses.

Once they both sat down, he looked kindly in her

eyes and with genuine concern on his face he asked her, "So my dear lady, what can I help you with? How can I be of assistance?"

"Well, I seemed to have attracted the same sort of life that I thought I left behind."

"I see, my dear." He pushed the pen and paper on the table toward her, "I want you to write down the story of your life. Note all your peaks and valleys, including how you felt about each experience, and each of your situations. I will see you at dinner time."

He abruptly stood up and took his leave of the room, slamming the door closed behind him. The sound of his footsteps got softer, the further he walked away. She was surprised by his abruptness as he left her there in solitude to reflect upon her life.

The day passed and evening came. Elizabeth Rose had several pages written by the time the keeper returned and brought her dinner. He was retiring for the night, and stated that in the morning they would review her story.

Elizabeth Rose was apprehensive, yet anticipatory as she snuggled in to bed. She felt she was on track to letting her past go and plotting out a positive future for herself.

Echoes of the keeper walking about the power plant woke Elizabeth Rose at sunbreak. Steam whistles went off and she heard clanking of wrenches and hammers from a distance. Soon the keeper's footsteps came closer to her door. She waited in trepidation.

He brought her breakfast and as she ate, he reviewed her story taking note of certain words she used and situations she described as being positive or negative. Then with these key words highlighted, he asked Elizabeth Rose to follow him.

She followed him through the winding staircases of the power plant. As they turned the corner, she saw the interior side of the paddle wheel spinning gently as the propulsion of the water moved it forward. She noticed that each of the pie shaped structural supports were color coded and had the words of key emotions on them such as joy, fear, sadness, and anger. A slight dribble sound could be heard as the scoop of the paddle took up water and the excess water dripped off. The color corresponding to the emotion would light as well. As the wheel slowly churned around, the illuminated emotion color would slowly fade.

The keeper shared with her that each basic emotion had a basic opposite and that these could combine to form advance emotions too. Elizabeth noticed the advance emotions written on the outer ring of the water paddle wheel.

The keeper began to explain the wheel, "Notice on the wheel how all the words have an opposite. Love has its remorse, joy has its sadness and optimism has its disappointment." Echoes of the wheel churning flooded the background. Gentle swishing noises were heard as the paddle picked up water in its buckets that circulated around the wheel and then gently escaped back into the river.

"Your emotions affect your energy, what you project out from your internal energy centers. Remember what your friend, Jade shared with you on the chi, qi or prana and the chakras?"

Elizabeth Rose nodded her head to acknowledge him.

"Notice how the colors of emotions relate to the chakra centers." He continued, "In all of life, each has its opposites. Black has its white. Red has its Green. Blue has its yellow. Female has its male. Day has its night. Sun has its moon. It's your task to find the balance, the Yin and Yang so that you can best maneuver life and find your balance, achieve all you desire."

Elizabeth Rose recalled that Jade had told her about the Yin and Yang of Taoism and Confucianism. How opposite or contrary forces were interconnected or interdependent in the natural world.

He sensed from her story that she had a lot of residual hurt, resulting from sadness and disappointment from the events in her life. The outcomes she experienced were not expected and surprised her, leaving her with feelings of disgust, envy and jealousy. Her goal was to turn these events into feelings of love, joy and optimism. He suggested to her to go back up to her room and in any areas she still felt hurt, he asked her to write out the pluses and minuses of the situation telling her that he would review them with her later.

At about noon, she heard the melodic whistling of the keeper coming closer to the guest room. He had Elizabeth Rose's lunch with him and as she ate he continued on with her lessons.

"In the story of your life, the negative events are ones you need to forgive." He schooled her, "Once forgiveness is achieved and accepted, the influence of these events ceases to exist. In order to move forward, you need to find the key to cause the click that unlocks the lingering anger and hurt, what you

121

are frustrated with. Then you have to implement the catalyst of change. The 'I am going to do this' and 'Doing this gives me joy'. Your moving to California was part of that catalyst of change. Your decision, 'I am going to California' and then actually doing it, was all part of the metamorphous. You then met the solider who opened up your heart to romantic love and what that could be like. Although you weren't sure about the whole area of romance, you still opened up your heart and experienced as much as you could with this man."

"And I want it again, but I'm afraid."

"Yes, but now your love is hurting you and that's not how love is supposed to be. It is like you built a fortress around your heart and you are not letting anyone in. The only ones you are attracting are the ones you do not want. That's causal power."

"You need to continue to analyze these negative events in your life and start to make them better. Start by fully grasping what role you played in them. What put you in that situation? Was it your choice, or life circumstances? Did you listen to someone else that put you in that situation or did you listen to yourself and your own inner guidance, what your heart told you to do? People can help you and can help you see a different point of view but don't let them make the decision for you."

Sitting across from her at the table, he looked her squarely in the eyes, "Now that you are an adult, rule number one is to always listen to you." He pointed at her with his index finger for emphasis, "You, yourself."

He pointed to the archetypes written on the wall. "And you also need to know the role you played in these various situations and your personality in social and intimate settings. So start by knowing yourself. Then there are a few other things I want you to do as well."

He pointed to her notepad, "You have already started to write the pluses and minuses of each situation, of each outcome. What was the plus for you in that situation and what was a minus? Then I want you to write from the perspective of the other parties involved, their point of view, pluses and minuses of the situation. There are at least three sides to every story and sometimes by looking at it from someone else's point-of-view; we gain a new perspective on the situation and events that occurred."

"Then we need to analyze the emotions involved. Fear and anger can be two very powerful emotions. If used properly, these two emotions can accelerate and propel you forward. They are both very powerful energies. If used negatively, they can put you behind, struggling in moving forward with living a fulfilling life."

"Remember how fear helped you get your younger sisters out of the house fire? Then how you feared Uncle Samuel, and how you worried about how you would deal with him once Cousin John had gone into the Army, leading to your decision to go to California? In these two instances, fear propelled you forward."

"Also recall how you were quick to anger with the goose on the farm. You learned your lesson very quickly on not being quick to anger. For a brief few minutes you experienced extreme regret. This changed your life forever and how you react to nasty beings."

"Typically, when we begin to be at peace with the events in our life, when we reflect back, we realize that everything in our life was meant to be, that we were right on track. Your reactions to the events determine your progression and your path."

He pointed to some words written on the wall and spoke them out loud.

"Clear Contradictions and Create Congruence."

Those events that you forgive and release will no longer hold you back. But if you hang on to them, they will deter you from moving forward, unable to break free from the emotional chains that bind you. Once you truly forgive, you will forget and move onward. Life was meant to be easy, not hard."

"If you are still having difficulty, then I want you to do a type of focused mediation. Spend some time in a quiet place where you can relax. Have pen and paper close by and ask yourself a question, but ask it in your heart, not in your head. Always come from a place of love. The energy of love is strong and true. Once you ask the question then wait for a response. Don't try to over analyze the information coming in, just accept it. It may seem a little far off at first, but as the information continues to unfold, the whole picture may make sense to you."

"If you get stuck or don't feel anything coming to you, then let it go. The universe has heard your question and will get back to you. Maybe get outside and go for a walk in nature. While here, walk amongst the grounds the power house, observe the trees and flowers, the birds, and wild life scooting about. Sit by the koi fish pond. Remember how you used to go off by yourself to the fields when you were in foster care? And how Jade shared with you the wisdom of the Buddha to be in present time?"

"Yes" she confirmed.

"You were practicing reflective meditation, but you need to take it a step further. Instead of feeling sorry for yourself, try to find the answers. Breathe in the fresh air and feel the gentle breeze of the mountain winds caress your face. Listen to the rustle of the leaves blowing in the wind and the chirp of the birds. Observe the butterflies fluttering about. Relax with the warmth of the sun against your face. Once you are relaxed, then maybe ponder your questions again, 'I wish to overcome this particular situation. What do I need to understand?'"

"While you are here, I will help you, but once you are home and you get stuck, then seek the help of a friend or some other outside assistance whether professional mainstream avenues or alternative practices. Is it past life regression or a more traditional therapist approach that you are drawn to? Follow your heart on what is the best to help you at that time. Once you pick a path, ask them to read your story or share with them the situation you are struggling with and ask them what they think about your perspective on the situation. Sometimes that person will see a point of view or think of an option that you never considered."

"Pay attention to your dreams during this time, for your higher consciousness may communicate to you through them and they may hold valuable clues. Ask your higher self, before you go to sleep at night, to help you understand a situation you are struggling with. Pay attention to books you are drawn to, repetitive news stories or magazine articles you come across. Or if a song is stuck in your head at a particular verse it could be your subconscious mind trying to tell you something. There is most likely something contained in them that is appropriate for you in your current life. If it doesn't resound with you right away, it may in a day or two, maybe even a week or two later. It may only be a brief experience of this unexpected knowledge. It may not be of major significance, but the point is that you followed your inner guidance; your inner knowing that directed you to follow through on a given task. That you received your answer."

"Your friend Jade was a seeker of truth and she sought it out in several ways. You shared in your life story how she had so much knowledge of different world's religions. Jade did whatever it took so she would understand and become at peace. She found comfort in recalling her times spent with her husband and in wearing the jade necklace he had given her. She believed that on some level, he was still a part of her in this life even though he was deceased."

"For love has many aspects; it can be expressed as simply as a display of respect or in the form of affection. You didn't always have the loving home life you wanted, but you had glimpses of it and now you are in a position where you can create that for your own family, in your life now."

The keeper pointed to the plaque on the wall between the door and the window overlooking the valley below, "Elizabeth Rose, as you see, the riches in our life are not measured by monetary gains or one's position in life but by the richness of our forgiving character. Let go of the past, forgive so you can move forward and create the life you desire. When you believe it in your heart and your logical mind is in agreement, that's when the shift occurs and all the changes begin to happen. You may feel a click or have an 'ah ha' moment or it may feel like a weight has been lifted. You've achieved balance and harmony."

Elizabeth Rose had much to ponder. Her head was spinning from all the wisdom the keeper had shared with her. She found it difficult to drift off to sleep that night as she recounted all that he shared with her and as she thought about the roles she played in all her life experiences.

With the rise of a new morning, she heard the keeper whistling a different tune as he was coming closer to her door. He swung the door open, bearing a big smile on his face.

"Good morning, Elizabeth Rose," he greeted her. As he put her breakfast tray down on her table, he asked "How are you feeling today?"

"Ok, I guess," she sadly replied.

"Why are you so glum?" he inquired.

She began to poke at the fried eggs on the plate, "I just wish I could have done some things differently."

"Ah, Elizabeth. You forgot that I shared with you that you are right on track. All the events in your life have happened in their due time." He patted her on her head, "There's nothing to worry or be sad about."

He pulled out the other chair and sat down by her. "Today I have something fun for you to do."

She snapped her head up from her state of despair. Her frown turned to a slight smile, as she was excited at what he had planned for her.

He pushed his thick eye glasses up and then slid the pad of paper and pen towards her. Pointing with his index finger toward her, he said, "I want you to write your new life story."

She sat intently, listening to him.

"I want you to write your wildest dreams. The key to this exercise is, I want you to write in the present tense, using the words 'I am' as often as you can and as appropriate. You can put in some details but being general is often best."

"But, before you even scratch down one sentence," he pointed at her, "I want you to identify your values." He pointed his index finger to the list of values written on the wall. "What is important to you right now in your life, what principles do you need to live by? This is your heart talking to you."

He took out two sheets of paper. The first one he wrote 'Values' across the top then as he slid it under the other sheet, he began to explain, "Then, I want you to write what your goals are." He wrote across the top of the other sheet the word 'Goals'. These two concepts are closely aligned and will change over time. But you need to identify what your values are in order to achieve your goals in your life."

He then pointed to the sheets of paper, "I also want you to think about what your motivations are for these values and goals. Just note it off to the side of your goals. If your values and goals are not aligned and if they are not supported by positive motivation you will not be in harmony- you will not be happy."

"Once you have these two lists completed, then I want you to write your new life story. And I want you to write it in the present active tense, using the words 'I am'. When you go through this exercise, if when you write something and it doesn't ring true in your heart, it is something that is not in harmony. You will need to reevaluate what it is you are trying to achieve."

"Change isn't always easy. You have to put some thought into it, plus some effort. But you need to know where you want to go, then how you are going to get there. I had you first work on releasing what is holding you back and now you need to define what it is you want moving forward. That is what this is all about."

As he got up, he patted Elizabeth Rose on her shoulder. "Work a little bit on your two lists then go outside for a walk around the grounds. Empty your mind. Ask your higher self for assistance in painting the life for you. You do have a beautiful light inside you dear Elizabeth. Go listen to it."

Elizabeth Rose worked on her lists for a while and occasionally glanced out the window at the beautiful, blue-sky day. She was at a standstill in her list creation and knew she needed a brief break. Taking the keepers advice, she made her way outside for some reflective time and fresh air.

It was such a sunny, warm day that she comfortably meandered about the grounds, looking at all the statues and the plantings of various foliage, flowers and trees. She was amazed at the height of the water lotus flowers that dotted the plant shelf along with a smattering of other pond foliage. She noticed several koi fish hidden amongst the plants and saw occasional bubbles rise to the surface sending ripples out.

Lying down by the side of the pond, she dipped her finger in the water and created similar bubble ripple effects on the surface of the pond. She watched as the ripples spanned out across the otherwise smooth surface before dissipating. This rippling effect intrigued her. As she played with the water, she allowed her mind to wander. She thought about her life interactions with others and how each reaction created a ripple. It was in that moment she realized that all actions have consequences and that thoughts were actions too.

She jumped up, feeling elated and energized, ready to complete her lists of values and goals.

When Elizabeth Rose came back, she found that the power plant keeper had put in her guest room a painting easel with paper, paint brushes and water colors. The keeper left her a note, "Write your new story then paint your new life. Where do you want to be? Paint from the end, not the beginning."

POWERISMS

❋ **Power of Emotions:** Emotions in balance empower our intentions. Emotions interfere when out of balance. Acknowledging the source of an emotion in the extreme helps to neutralize the power of the emotion.

❋ **Causal Power:** What you unknowingly project out into the world is intrinsically responsible for what attracts back to you.

❋ **Power of Forgiveness:** Forgiveness is the catalyst to forgetting. If you haven't forgiven someone, it will be a stumbling block and prevent you in moving forward.

❋ **Power of Now:** Being present in thought stills the mind so the answers can come through.

❋ **Power of Change:** Change first occurs as a thought or idea, and then when combined with action can set a new course or direction for one's life; first in mind, then in reality.

❋ **Power of Intention:** Thought is the initial catalyst to change. Intention is the motion that puts that change in action. Using the words, "I am" is a powerful way to express an intention.

POWER TOOLS

✎ **Write your Life Story:** Once you write your life story, analyze it looking for key words such as negative emotions. Also, look for common themes or repetitive experiences for these are key areas to find a way to release, forgive and forget.

- **Know Yourself:** A process of clearing your contradictions and creating congruence in your life to reveal your balanced beauty.
- **Pluses & Minuses:** Write out the pluses and minuses of each negative situation in which you have unresolved undesirable emotions attached.
- **Three Sides:** Analyze the negative situations from the point of view of all parties involved, even those who were maybe just observers. Sometimes when we view from another's perspective it helps to see where we could have maybe changed a response to have a different outcome. From this viewpoint, it is then sometimes easier to forgive and forget.
- **Focused Meditation:** Find a quiet place to be alone and get centered. With pen and paper, think about what it is you seek an answer to or a solution. Be quiet. Let the thoughts or words come to you.
- **Listen to Yourself:** When you make a decision, always make sure you are listening to yourself and not making a decision based on someone else's desires or use their words. Everything should come 100% from you.
- **Examine and Prioritize Your Values:** Most times problems arise when our values are not in alignment with our decisions and the goals we have set for ourselves. These will need to be re-evaluated during the course of your life.

✎ **Set New Goals:** Your goals are closely aligned with your values. But if you don't know what your values are, in trying to obtain or once you do obtain your goals, balance will not be achieved. You will always be out of balance. You will set new goals throughout your lifetime.

✎ **Paint a New Picture:** This exercise aligns your values and goals giving you an action plan to achieve congruence so your true beauty can emerge.

✎ **Reflective Meditation:** This type of meditation is usually used to receive answers to questions. Walk in nature or do some activity in which you can put yourself in the 'now'. Be in present time; listen and observe nature, breathe deeply and relax. Once calm and in a clear mind, ask questions about what you have been struggling with or regarding the answers you are seeking.

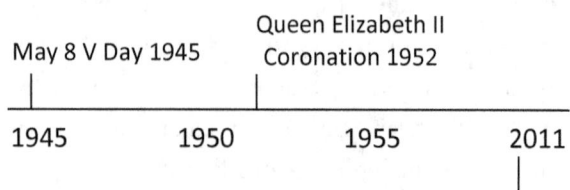

May 8 V Day 1945

Queen Elizabeth II
Coronation 1952

1945   1950   1955   2011

Prince William and Kate Middleton, Duchess of
Cambridge Marry - April 29, 2011

8 THE PAINTED PICTURE

Feeling inspired from her walk around the grounds, Elizabeth Rose sat down and immediately wrote out her new life story. She plotted out the steps she would take on the way to achieving all her desires. First and foremost for her, was that she wanted to create a loving home, like she had briefly experienced with her mother and then with Grandma and Grandpa Friedrich. Her husband had to share her values and want children. She thought of ways she could meet her future husband and ways she could realize if he shared her same values and goals in life.

She also wanted to work in a hospital. It was important to her to work in an environment that focused on helping people. She hadn't forgotten how nice and caring all the hospital staff were toward her when she had her appendix operation. She wasn't quite sure what she wanted to do there but she wasn't concerned about that for now.

Then she set about to painting her picture. She painted a house with a yard and a family out front with smiles on their faces. She painted herself wearing a type of uniform, such as someone in a hospital might wear and her husband in a military uniform. For some reason she thought of the handsome navy officer who knocked down the can display at the grocery store and she hoped that maybe one day she would see him again.

In the distance, she heard the whistling of the keeper bringing her lunch. She was proud for all she had accomplished that morning and couldn't wait to share it with him.

While she ate lunch, he scanned over her two lists of her values and goals. Periodically he remarked, "Very nice" and, "You got it." As he finished reading her story he commented, "Very well thought out." He smiled at her then looked at her picture, "Well done, you did a really good job." Elizabeth Rose was beaming inside.

"You see all this?" he questioned her as he motioned his hand around the room at the pages she had written and the painting she painted. "This is a life of purpose." He looked her squarely in her eyes, "Your purpose in life is to make you" he pointed at her, "happy."

A tingling sensation went down Elizabeth Rose's spine. It was as if time stopped and everything became crystal clear to her. She understood. She cleared her contradictions and created congruence.

It took some effort while she was there, but it wasn't hard. She realized that some of her repetitive experiences were put in her life because she drew them to herself and needed to recognize them to find a way to release them. She also realized how her life had been out of harmony when she wasn't living in alignment with her values and goals.

The keeper pointed to the quote by Neville Goddard written above the doorway and shared it out loud, "A change of feeling is a change in destiny."

Continuing on he said, "Remember you must first and foremost listen to yourself, to your heart, and your inner guidance. You need to take care of yourself first, and then the rest will follow. The power is inside you."

He stated as he pointed at her chest, "Your thoughts and beliefs shape your life. Your willingness to be the chief architect of your life versus being the victim makes all the difference in the castle you build to live in."

He continued, "Each day, I want you to plan your day."

Elizabeth Rose immediately began to take notes.

"Not just with what you will eat or who you will see, but in what you will do that day to bring your values into alignment with your daily life and achieve your goals."

He held up her values and goals lists. "This is what I value right now, and this is what I am going to do to achieve this goal. Then at night, when you express your appreciation for things that happened that day, also think about what you did or what you could have done better to live according to your values and achieving your goals."

He leaned back in his chair, "If there was something you could have done better, it could be that you have a belief that is not in alignment with your values and goals. Beliefs are very powerful in shaping our lives. What you believe to be true influences you on a daily basis. And if you say one thing and feel another, this is a strong clue that you are not operating in harmony with your beliefs. If this happens, go to your heart and ask, 'What is going on with me achieving this goal? What belief do I have that is holding me back?' Listen for the answers. The heart doesn't lie."

"I have something to show you." She followed him through the winding stair cases of the power plant again. As they turned the corner, she saw the interior side of the paddle wheel spinning gently as the propulsion of the water moved it forward. But something was different. She noticed that each of the pie shaped structural support segments had changed to the color of purple. The wheel churning echoed in the background. Gentle swishing noises were heard as the paddles buckets escaped its cleansed emotions, depositing the water into the Stream of Life. The recirculated water rushed forward as it left the paddle and joined the natural flow of the water currents.

In that moment she felt a release. A sense of cleansing and strength flushed through her body and mind like all sorts of emotional weights and burdens had been lifted. She felt a little tingly, as if she was electrified with new life, new energy, new thoughts and a new outlook on life. Her vibration had lifted up and she felt prepared and equipped to take on the next phase of her life challenges. With this new lease on life, she felt younger, invigorated and like a kid again.

The keeper let her take in the moment, to process and integrate all she was experiencing. When she was ready, she reached out to give him a long, loving hug of thanks. She knew it was time to go home.

As the keeper escorted Elizabeth Rose to the

outside of the power plant, he shared with her, "Sometimes when we take a different road to avoid our destiny, we find it."

She didn't quite understand what he was saying for she was still trying to comprehend and absorb all that she had learned from her brief visit. Her contemplation turned to elation at the sight of Old Mike who was waiting for her there. Her eyes opened wide and her mouth dropped at the sight of him. She eagerly ran up to hug her old faithful farm companion, throwing her arms around his neck. She looked into his eyes and stroked the side of his face, saying "I missed you, my true friend."

She pulled back to take him all in. It was Old Mike, but he was different. He was younger, more youthful looking. It was as if he regressed in years. His coat was a shiny, lustrous white that the sun's rays bounced off of and he had a horn coming out the center of his forehead. He was a unicorn now.

"Come on, up you go" the keeper pushed Elizabeth Rose forward and helped her on to Mike's back. As she sat up on Old Mike, she gazed down upon the keeper, with his thick, round-circle glasses and disheveled salt and pepper hair. His smiling blue eyes appeared as large as the lenses, due to the magnified strength of his glasses.

"Remember, a change in feeling is a change in destiny. Always look for joy." Elizabeth Rose reached down to hug him. As they pulled back he continued, "You are the power house" he said as he pointed his index finger at her. "Repeat after me, 'I am the power house.'"

As Elizabeth Rose began to repeat the phrase, "I am the power house" the keeper hit Old Mike on the back hind-quarter and he took off down the side of the mountain. Wings came out of his sides that Elizabeth Rose hadn't noticed before and together they glided down to the valley below.

Elizabeth Rose was tossing from side-to-side saying out loud, "I am the power house. I am the power house" when the blaring sound of BRRRRRRRRRRing interrupted her dreaming. Startled from her deep sleep, she grabbed the alarm clock to shut it off. The ice pack that was resting on her forehead fell to her lap and she reached her hand up to feel where the lump was. It was almost gone.

She reclined back a moment to recall her dream. And ponder what role the keeper played in it. He had her analyze her life then put down what it was she wanted. She then became the keeper of her life. She thought about all the things he had her do, like write her life story then analyze it looking for negative emotions and repetitive experiences. Next he had her write out the pluses and minuses of each situation and the different perspectives of those involved.

At this point she searched her night stand for paper to write some of the things down. She couldn't believe how powerful the dream was and she wanted to remember as much of it as she could so she could actually do it when she got home from work that evening.

Her mind was racing and her hand was trying to keep up writing out all the memories of the thoughts and concepts from the dream. Tick, tock, tick, tock went her wind up alarm clock that was sitting on the nightstand. She was stressing. She wanted to write down as much as she could but she had to stop. She didn't want to be late for work.

All the while she got ready, different segments of the dream popped to mind. She finally went to her stand to grab the paper and jot some of the memories down. With each minute she was awake, the more she recalled her dream, the more she felt uplifted.

In the bathroom, she laughed when she saw in the mirror the purple bruised bump on her forehead. But inside she felt it was all worth it for the insightful dream she had last night.

She was definitely running late as she scampered into the kitchen. There would be no time to make breakfast or a sack lunch. The negativity of the Egyptian bowl with the gloves and Douglas MacArthur pin in it stopped her in her tracks. There was no way she wanted those items left in her house for one more day as she found a grocery bag to put the items in. With the paper bag and her purse in hand, she took a couple cookies with her, then ran out the door to catch the bus to work.

Luckily the bus was just pulling up. She paid her fare and found a seat. Her mind wanted to recirculate the dream again but people were a buzz about the Allied push into Germany. She saw the headlines on the newspapers people were holding. The Allies were expected to declare victory against the Nazi aggression shortly.

For a while, she took in the conversations that were going on around her about the celebrations then switched her thoughts to her dream. What she came away with most strongly from it was that she needed to focus daily on the positive things that happened in her life and find things to do that brought her joy. She also needed to date someone else and he must share her values. Then it seemed that everything else she desired would most likely fall into place.

She arrived at Kroger with an upbeat demeanor and a new perspective on life. Everyone in the store was in a jovial mood. The manager and Viola could see that something inside Elizabeth Rose had changed and they were glad to see the cloud of sadness had lifted from her. She radiated an inner beauty and an outer beauty that was very magnetic. She was in balance and harmony with those around her. The customers seemed more drawn to her and wanted to engage in conversation. Her demeanor was a powerful calm.

With the noon time rush over, Elizabeth Rose decided to go across the street to the little diner to eat lunch. The place was crammed with tables and booths one upon another and for some reason today, it was jammed with customers even though it was nearly 1:30pm. She was lucky to get a booth by the windows that had just opened up. The waitress promptly brought her a glass of water and a menu which she immediately began to study. Her two cookies had left her many hours earlier and she was hungry.

A steady stream of people seemed to be constantly walking by her booth in between the line of tables. It was the main walkway in the restaurant. From the corner of her eye she caught a man who stopped next to her table.

"Why hello" he greeted her. She jerked her head up from the menu. "Mind if I join you?"

It was him- the naval officer. Elizabeth Rose's heart got fluttery and started to race.

"Hi" she greeted him back, "Please do."

He took his hat off and laid it on the seat next to him, "I'm Chief Petty Officer Pierson. But you can call me Jack. And who do I have the pleasure of meeting?"

She extended her hand to shake his and sweetly shared, "I'm Elizabeth Rose." The gentle grip of his handshake combined with his suntan skin and bleached blonde, crew cut hair, made his hazel eyes dance off his face, and sent shivers down her spine.

"It's a pleasure to meet you."

"Same to you. So what do you do for the Navy?"

"I train junior officers."

"Are you from here?"

"Yes, I am. Actually I was born in Yucaipa, California. And you?"

"Wisconsin. I just moved out here about a year ago."

"Wow, all the way from Wisconsin. Why here?"

"My best friend from high school got a teaching job out here and she invited me to come along."

"I see. I always wanted to go to Milwaukee and Chicago. I thought it would be neat to see a baseball game at Wrigley field. And I hear those Green Bay Packers are quite the tough football team that I'd like to see play sometime too."

"Hi Hun," the waitress greeted Jack, as she set down a glass of water for him. "Can I take your orders?"

Elizabeth Rose offered him the menu. He put his hand up, "I'm a regular here. Ladies first."

"And you dear?" the waitress asked.

"I will have a bowl of the chicken dumpling soup and a hamburger please."

"Anything to drink?"

"A Coca Cola" Elizabeth Rose added.

Jack confirmed, "The usual, meatloaf and black coffee please"

"You never made it back into the grocery store."

"Well, as you can tell I'm not much of a cook." He chuckled, "I didn't even have to look at the menu." He shrugged his shoulders and looked at his light khaki shirt, "I spend all my free time ironing." His comment was to poke fun at himself for his class C service uniform, which was neatly pressed.

"Nor a walker," Elizabeth Rose teased him.

He smiled with her having made fun at the expense of him, "Yeah, I don't know my way around a grocery store too well. But an iron, that's a different story."

"Oh, I hate to iron. With me being at ease in a grocery store and you being so good at ironing, we'd make a good team."

Their conversation continued to easily flow as they enjoyed their meals and their conversation together. There was a particular magnetism about Elizabeth Rose that Jack found hard to define. When he first saw her in Kroger, he was initially drawn to her outer beauty, but the more they conversed he was pulled in by an inner beauty of calmness and confidence that she exuded. They talked about how the Nazi aggression seemed to be finally contained in Europe but the Japanese still were posing a threat. The more they talked, the more he was drawn in by her confidence. It was an inner calm she was powerfully radiating. She had a balanced beauty that he wanted in his life too.

When the waitress came with the check, Jack

promptly took it from her and immediately placed a tip on the table.

Elizabeth Rose blushed. She was smitten with his charm, his good looks and his manners. "Thank you so much for lunch, Jack. I really enjoyed talking to you."

"Me too," Jack smiled. Inside, he was bursting at the seams with exhilaration, feeling like he would just die if he didn't see her again.

"Are you free to go see Benny Goodman this Saturday night?"

Elizabeth Rose beamed inside. "Why yes, I am."

"Great, where can I pick you up?"

Like Jade had shared how Queen Elizabeth I charted out a new course for her empire, Elizabeth Rose charted out a new course for her life. Her decision to move to California set in place a chain of life-changing events. Working for the Pisoniano's was a stepping stone which helped her transition her life there, but it was a repetitive experience she needed to break. The job at Kroger gave her smooth sailing waters to plot out a new course even with the loss of Tom Krol.

Her power plant dream set in motion an internal understanding and identified additional changes she needed to make which alleviated the stress and strain that was holding her back. She realized she was out of alignment with her internal desires and it was affecting her externally. She emerged with a new perspective that caused her to emit a magnetic beauty of calm and confidence. She had direction and control in her life.

Soon after her enlightening power plant dream, the concentration camp prisoners were freed and V-Day declared. Elizabeth Rose realized that with all she had endured in her life, nothing compared to the emotional damage inflicted on the camp survivors during the few short years of the war.

The end of WWII saw an economic rebirth in the U.S. economy. Elizabeth Rose married Navy Petty Officer Jack Pierson in the summer of 1946. Grandma and Grandpa Friedrich made their first trip to California, just for her wedding to Jack.

Jack became her shipmate for life. With him she found a loving partner who shared similar values and goals and gave her life stability. Soon after the wedding they purchased a bungalow and started their family.

Elizabeth Rose left her positon at the Kroger grocery store with the arrival of her first born child. She kept in contact with Viola occasionally over the years and it was nice to hear how the rest of the staff was doing from her. Elizabeth Rose was very appreciative of the kindness extended to her during her employment there. Once the children were in school full days, Elizabeth Rose then fulfilled one of her other goals and transitioned into work at a local hospital.

Elizabeth Rose still saw Rae periodically over the years. They were witnesses at each other's weddings. Rae married Frank and together they raised their families in the same neighborhood.

With the housing boom that followed after WWII, Grandpa Friedrich had left the lumber company and started his own construction company. His knowledge of barn and home building, plus his experience as a scaler at the lumber company, and running a farm was the perfect background to build a successful construction business. He even expanded into commercial masonry and stone construction, including building banks.

On Grandma and Grandpa Friedrich's last trip to California, Grandpa Friedrich expanded Elizabeth Rose and Jack's home to have an additional bedroom and bathroom. It was needed for their expanding family.

Occasional family trips were taken back to Wisconsin. Jack loved planning the route and did most of the driving. He often planned the trips so they were able to see her Cousin John and his family.

John and his wife opened up a saloon in Jackson Hole, Wyoming and called it 'The Two-Bit Watering Hole'. It was John's subtle way of poking back at his deceased father by opening up a cheap saloon with the money he inherited and incorporating his father's favorite abusive saying in the name of the business. He shared with Elizabeth Rose that with the time his father spent in bars, there must be some money to be made in owning one. He joked with her that his first choice to name the bar was SOB, as a jab at his deceased father, Samuel Ordel Blackmore. But after consideration, he thought only people that caused trouble would come and he didn't want to have a daily reminder of him.

Cousin John and Elizabeth Rose had a bond that when they saw each other it was just like no time had passed. They often regressed to reminiscing about life on the farm, but they knew it was best to let bygones be bygones. They had better lives now and put their painful past behind them.

While visiting in Wisconsin, Elizabeth Rose and Jack stayed with Grandma and Grandpa Friedrich until their passing then Aunt Annabel and her family. Annabel had married a man who worked in a factory and had a life of her own now.

When Elizabeth Rose, Jack and their family visited, Grandma and Grandpa Friedrich would often hold a celebratory gathering in which all the family and friends were invited. Bobby often attended with his wife and children. He moved back after his time served in the Army, married a girl a couple years younger and secured work at one of the area paper mills. He still held a special affection for Elizabeth Rose and would love to steal a minute of her time at these gathers just for them to talk.

After dinner, the instruments were pulled out for the evening entertainment. Elizabeth Rose was still grandpa's little Totsy. He loved to call her and Jack out to dance. It put a twinkle in his eye to see the lovely woman she had become.

Libations steadily flowed, although things would quiet down at the party. The men often gathered around the dining table playing cards while the women cleaned up and conversed in the kitchen. It was often near midnight when these gatherings ended.

Eventually, all the relatives made the rounds to visit or Elizabeth Rose and Jack paid them a call. Tetty and Tulla both married and had families of their own. Aunt Emmy and her husband still had a small farm. Aunt Evie sold the farm when Uncle Samuel passed then moved to town to work at a restaurant.

Elizabeth Rose was able to see Jade on a couple of

her trips back to Wisconsin although they talked weekly up until her death. She was so proud to introduce Jack to Jade. Jade was right, she would have a loving partner and stable family of her own, just like Jade had with her husband.

Elizabeth Rose was sitting back in her cushioned recliner watching the wedding news coverage of Kate Middleton to Prince William. She reflected how all along Jade was right, that you could achieve anything you desired, that you just needed to put yourself where you wanted to be in order to have the opportunity to achieve your dreams. But also, as she saw Kate go through the short breakup her and Prince William had, she knows that a person has to sometimes sort things through in order to move forward.

For Elizabeth Rose that sorting through came for her during her time of transition out in California. Unbeknownst to her, her life paralleled the U.S. war effort in which America went from a 3rd rate county to a superpower. Her turning point coincided with her realization that her continued employment at the Pisoniano household was equivalent to being an American ship at sea, helpless to defend itself against a Japanese kamikaze attack.

She witnessed President Roosevelt overcome the debilitating paralysis effects of polio, to rise up and lead the country into a defensive battle against hostile aggression by other countries.

Her war was to take charge of her life and to make peace with the things that she found so hard to forgive and forget them such as the physical abuse by Uncle Samuel and the farm foster families she worked so hard for in which she wasn't acknowledge or shown any appreciation for her work. Although she didn't have time to out maneuver and escape the trap set by Miriam, Floyd and Mr. Pisoniano, afterwards, she was able to chart a new course for her life.

Similar to the Allied war effort having its inspirational and guiding leaders of FDR and Churchill, Elizabeth Rose had Jade and the power plant keeper. Although Elizabeth Rose didn't become a princess as she dreamt when she was a child, she did become the ruler of her kingdom by the wisdom she learned from them. As Lady Elizabeth had been schooled in areas relevant to being a leader and ruler, Elizabeth Rose was shown by Jade and the keeper of the power plant that she had the power to set the direction of her life, to protect her personal kingdom as well as how to rise above life changing or challenging events. She achieved all she wanted in life and fulfilled her life purpose by making herself happy. She was alright with that in her heart.

POWERISMS

❋ **Power of Living from the End:** It's where your focus is on a daily basis, to achieve what it is you desire. Your emotions and values, plus your goals, must all be in alignment. The feelings associated with joy are most beneficial as well, for success to occur.

❋ **Power of Belief:** Belief is the foundation that shapes our lives influencing our values and goals. Your thoughts and feelings must be in agreement in order for a belief to form.

❋ **Power of Resilience:** An individual that is resilient thrives or bounces back quickly during difficult times. The key is harnessing a neutral-positive outlook which deactivates any possibilities of negative effects (emotionally and physically).

❋ **Power of Balanced Beauty:** When emotions, values and goals are in alignment, balanced beauty is achieved; happiness occurs, peace and contentment is projected. Your inner beauty and outer beauty are merged. You express a magnetism that is your true beauty.

POWER TOOLS

🔧 **Taking Your Power Back:** A combination of an individual's self-analysis, self-respect, making value-based decisions and taking action to achieve goals which results in your balanced beauty.

Plan Daily Action: Put in motion what you have plotted out, frame your desired outcomes and gauge your progress daily.

9 SUMMARY OF POWERISMS AND POWER TOOLS

These Powerisms and Power Tools are elaborated upon in materials used by the author as part of an online coaching course found at cbhe-online.com, and in an accompanying workbook (ISBN 978-0-9960945-1-1) which at this time of publication is offered as part of an individual coaching program or workshops.

DEFINITIONS

Powerisms are concepts that are full of force or energy. They are active and potent and influence an individual on many levels such as physical, mental and emotional and often times have more than one aspect. **Power Tools** are actions that can be taken to positively propel or influence an individual to move forward in achieving their goals.

CHAPTER 1 PASS THE TOTSY
POWERISMS

- **Power of Love:** Loving influences can shape your life. Through love you can positively influence another's life. You should always come from a place of love. Sometimes other forces are at work and love just isn't enough.

- **Power of Fear:** Fear can hold you back or propel you forward in times of distress. It can also protect you.

- **Power of Survival:** Any event you survive gives you more references to draw upon. Sometimes you repeat experiences until you learn. With each experience, you accumulate strength and stamina.

- **Power to Heal:** Just being in the presence of someone who offers unconditional love can heal. People can heal themselves too through meditative prayers or in changing their health habits.

- **Power of the Heart:** Your heart is most powerful at manifesting and is intricately connected to your mind and to a higher knowing. When the decision is made to follow the heart, it is usually the correct decision.

- **Power of Anger:** Anger can change a person's life forever. An individual needs to control their response to mitigate the possible negative repercussions of the outcome. If the response is done hastily, as in a reaction without thought, it can cause regret.

POWER TOOLS

Appreciation: Find something each day to be appreciative for in a way that easily incorporates into your daily routine. Each thing you are grateful for is a blessing. This simple practice gives your life a sense of fulfillment and signals the universe to send you more blessings.

Creative Expression: Creative activities can include dancing, laughing, hanging out with friends, painting or anything creative that allows your mind to shift focus and the answers to come through. These activities instill a sense of joy while reducing stress and anxiety.

CHAPTER 2 JADE
POWERISMS

Power of Words: Written and spoken words can set the direction of one's life, either positively or negatively and most definitely affects others on a daily basis.

Power of Thoughts: Thoughts can be the catalyst to change. Some repetitive thoughts are a lesson to be learned. Once the lesson is learned the thoughts cease. Repetitive thoughts, if not controlled can causally effect outcomes. The best thoughts to think are those that help you feel joy.

Power of Unconditional Love: Unconditional love is the strongest power there is and is most often used to support others.

❋ **Power of Energy:** We are all energetically connected. Every action has energy. Every individual should be conscious of this, for their actions always impact themselves and others. Choose your thoughts, words and actions wisely, for they can permanently impact your destiny or another's.

❋ **Power to Influence:** Every interaction you have with others influences your life and theirs. Choose your words and actions wisely.

❋ **Power of Conscious Creation:** All answers are inside each person. Key components to your ability to consciously create include watching your thoughts and eliminating emotional contradictions which are not in congruence with your values. Don't look to others for answers, for their energy can interfere with yours. Your moto should be, "Don't go out, go in." When all is in congruence such as thoughts, emotions, values, actions, etc., your true, balanced beauty emerges.

POWER TOOLS

🔨 **Power of Cleaning and Clearing:** Revaluate your relationships to identify disharmonies with your values and goals. Remove any objects that have emotional attachments of hurt associated with them. Clean up any areas of clutter as these also distract the mind. Eliminating negative visual cues allows your mind to easily focus on things positively.

🔨 **Power of Imagination:** This needs to be practiced with care. Choose thoughts, words and outcomes carefully because, ultimately, what you think and feel, you create.

CHAPTER 3 CROSSING THE THRESHOLD
POWERISMS

✸ **Power of Dreams:** Achieving dreams requires plotting and planning. Words, thoughts and imagination play an important role and must be chosen wisely.

✸ **Power of Self-Respect:** It's a form of self-love, self-belief and self-worth. By not imposing boundaries in how others treat you, you invite a lack of respect. Have empathy for others but don't allow others to take advantage of you.

✸ **Power of Time:** Time allows one to see a different perspective which can lead to life-changing decisions.

✸ **Abuse of Power:** Power when abused is the exertion of unnecessary control or manipulation of other individuals for one's own personal gain. The ego is usually involved and eventually these actions by the abuser sets them back from anything they thought they gained by their controlling, manipulative actions.

POWER TOOLS

🔨 **Expressing One's Self:** Take time to express your feelings along with your desired new outcome when you are repeatedly experiencing frustrating situations.

🔨 **Making Decisions:** When decisions are made, this sets in motion other events in one's life.

CHAPTER 4 EL CAPTAIN
POWERISIMS

✹ **Power of an Open Heart:** Sometimes your desires are presented to you in a slightly different format and the challenge will be to recognize and accept that which is presented to you as fulfilling that desire, that goal. An open heart is flexible and accepting.

✹ **Power of Going with the Flow:** Sometimes positive outcomes can happen just with going with the flow of life. Other times, if no conscious effort is put into life events, it can leave one feeling as a victim of circumstances.

POWER TOOLS

🔨 **Power of Action:** Desire (motivation and emotion) propels an individual into action. Once a decision is made, your action is the steps taken to achieve a goal which is supported by a value. Action sets in motion change, and sets an individual on a new path.

🔨 **Power of Risks:** Sometimes caution must be thrown to the wind and action taken to propel you on your way to achieving a desired outcome.

CHAPTER 5 BELLY OF THE WHALE
POWERISMS

❋ **Power of Repetitive Experiences:** Experiences are repeated until the lesson is learned. Often times, all you need to do is recognize the pattern and when in the circumstance again, decline to get involved or take action to separate from the situation.

❋ **Power of Thought as Initial Catalyst:** Any intuitive, spontaneous thought can protect you as in times of possible harm, or propel you forward and open new doors of opportunity for you. However, negative self-talk, whether thought or even if just spoken "off the cuff', can hold you back and hinder your progression. Listen to your own internal guidance and watch you words!

POWER TOOL

🔩 **Change in Feelings:** When your feelings change, it can set in motion a new direction for your life. It is a sign that you have a new desire. Action is required to harmonize your values with your change in emotions and new goals.

CHAPTER 6 LIFE OF PURPLE
POWERISMS

❋ **Power of Desire:** Desire is based in an emotion and is an urge that leads to change. Something is lacking in your life and signals there will be realignment of an emotion, value or goal.

❃ **Power of Challenges:** When determination is used to overcome challenges, life changes occur. Could be a way to alert you to choose another path.

❃ **Power of Exercise:** Exercise puts your mind on a different focus, allowing things to be processed in the background and solutions to develop. Also, exercise releases endorphins that improve a person's mood state.

POWER TOOL

✎ **Power of Imposter Self:** It's the negative internal voice that tells you you're not good enough, or that you can't succeed. It comes from a fear of failure or rejection and may be based on a past event. An individual may not realize they have these sabotaging, self-defeating thoughts. Once recognized, a change in mindset can be implemented including use of words and thoughts that support this change, along with action and risk taking to not only achieve a desired outcome but deactivate this negative internal voice.

CHAPTER 7 MEETING THE POWER PLANT KEEPER
POWERISMS

❃ **Power of Emotions:** Emotions in balance empower our intentions. Emotions interfere when out of balance. Acknowledging the source of an emotion in the extreme helps to neutralize the power of the emotion.

❀ **Causal Power:** What you unknowingly project out into the world is intrinsically responsible for what attracts back to you.

❀ **Power of Forgiveness:** Forgiveness is the catalyst to forgetting. If you haven't forgiven someone, it will be a stumbling block and prevent you in moving forward.

❀ **Power of Now:** Being present in thought stills the mind so the answers can come through.

❀ **Power of Change:** Change first occurs as a thought or idea, and then when combined with action can set a new course or direction for one's life; first in mind, then in reality.

❀ **Power of Intention:** Thought is the initial catalyst to change. Intention is the motion that puts that change in action. Using the words, "I am" is a powerful way to express an intention.

POWER TOOLS

🔨 **Write your Life Story:** Once you write your life story, analyze it looking for key words such as negative emotions. Also, look for common themes or repetitive experiences for these are key areas to find a way to release, forgive and forget.

🔨 **Know Yourself:** A process of clearing contradictions and creating congruence in your life to reveal your balanced beauty.

🔨 **Pluses & Minuses:** Write out the pluses and minuses of each negative situation in which you have unresolved undesirable emotions attached.

🔨 **Three Sides:** Analyze the negative situations from the point of view of all parties involved, even those who were maybe just observers. Sometimes when we view from another's perspective it helps to see where we could have maybe changed a response to have a different outcome. From this viewpoint, it is then sometimes easier to forgive and forget.

🔨 **Focused Meditation:** Find a quiet place to be alone and get centered. With pen and paper, think about what it is you seek an answer to or a solution. Be quiet. Let the thoughts or words come to you.

🔨 **Listen to Yourself:** When you make a decision, always make sure you are listening to yourself and not making a decision based on someone else's desires or use their words. Everything should come 100% from you.

🔨 **Examine and Prioritize Your Values:** Most times problems arise when our values are not in alignment with our decisions and the goals we have set for ourselves. These will need to be re-evaluated during the course of your life.

🔨 **Set New Goals:** Your goals are closely aligned with your values. But if you don't know what your values are, in trying to obtain or once you do obtain your goals, balance will not be achieved.

You will always be out of balance. You will set new goals throughout your lifetime.

🔨 **Paint a New Picture:** This exercise aligns your values and goals giving you an action plan to achieve congruence so your true beauty can emerge.

🔨 **Reflective Meditation:** This type of meditation is usually used to receive answers to questions. Walk in nature or do some activity in which you can put yourself in the 'now'. Be in present time; listen and observe nature, breathe deeply and relax. Once calm and in a clear mind, ask questions about what you have been struggling with or regarding the answers you are seeking.

CHAPTER 8 THE PAINTED PICTURE POWERISMS

🌸 **Power of Living from the End:** It's where your focus is on a daily basis, to achieve what it is you desire. Your emotions and values, plus your goals, must all be in alignment. The feelings associated with joy are most beneficial as well, for success to occur.

🌸 **Power of Belief:** Belief is the foundation that shapes our lives influencing our values and goals. Your thoughts and feelings must be in agreement in order for a belief to form.

🌸 **Power of Resilience:** An individual that is resilient thrives or bounces back quickly during difficult times. Key is harnessing a neutral-positive outlook which deactivates any possibilities of negative effects (emotionally and physically).

❋ **Power of Balanced Beauty:** When emotions, values and goals are in alignment, balanced beauty is achieved; happiness occurs, peace and contentment is projected. Your inner beauty and outer beauty are merged. You express a magnetism that is your true beauty.

POWER TOOLS

🔨 **Taking Your Power Back:** A combination of an individual's self-analysis, self-respect, making value-based decisions and taking action to achieve goals which results in your balanced beauty.

🔨 **Plan Daily Action:** Put in motion what you have plotted out, frame your desired outcomes and gauge your progress daily.

PAINTED PICTURE

Congruence = Balanced Beauty	
Make Decisions	Eliminate Contradictions
1. Listen to Yourself 2. Honor Your Values 3. Remain Focused	• Neutralize Emotions • Changes in Feeling • Mind Chatter
Thoughts, Words, Action, Belief	
Imagination, Dreams	
Goals & Values	

ABOUT THE AUTHOR

Ginger Glomstead has been a presenter and educator for most of her career and is hypnosis certified. She is a published author of two books specific to the beauty industry, *Common Disorders of the Skin, Scalp and Hair: A Quick Reference for Licensed Beauty Professionals,* and *Understanding Common Dermatitis and the FDAs Role in Cosmetics,* which she offers with continuing education classes for licensed beauty professionals. She has also written a screen play, *The Boy In Green* and a contemporary romance novel, *Spinning a Good Yarn.*

With this fictional self-help endeavor, she further expands her creative writing and educational offerings. She currently has a fictional trilogy project in process, a family saga based in the beauty industry (*Living Large: The Rise, Icon, Legacy*). To follow this author's works, please visit www.GKGlomstead.com.

GINGER K. GLOMSTEAD

Every effort was given to edit this work. To report any errors, please report them through the author website, www.GKGlomstead.com, on the "Contact Us" tab.